Hard Sell

Marc S. Blevins

authorHOUSE™

1663 LIBERTY DRIVE, SUITE 200
BLOOMINGTON, INDIANA 47403
(800) 839-8640
WWW.AUTHORHOUSE.COM

First published by AuthorHouse 11/14/05

ISBN: 1-4208-7443-8 (sc)
ISBN: 1-4208-7445-4 (dj)

Library of Congress Control Number: 2005909957

Printed in the United States of America
Bloomington, Indiana

This book is printed on acid-free paper.

1

The words from the Eagles' "Hotel California" wafted up to the rafters as I sat at the bar and worked my way through my third gin and tonic. The windows to the deck were open and a breeze came in from the beach across the street. I had been in Rhode Island for a total of forty-seven minutes, and so far I liked it.

The door to my right opened, and as I glanced up, a young blond walked through the entrance and made her way over to the bar. She was wearing a polka-dotted sundress, and had on heels that only accentuated her already strong calves. She had full, pouty lips that framed a set of teeth that must've cost her about three thousand dollars. I could tell because as she sat down, she smiled, and of course, she flashed her smile at me.

I had been in Rhode Island for a total of forty-eight minutes, and I was liking it even more.

Before I was able to open my mouth and inform her of all the wonderful things she was about to learn about me, the blond's shoulder was draped with an incredibly large, fleshy hand which was, in turn, attached to an immense arm. I followed the path of the arm up to its shoulder, and saw that it connected with a body that rippled with obesity. Blond Girl tore her gaze away from me, and turned and kissed the fleshy cheek of the fleshy head that rested atop this mountainous monstrosity.

Forty-nine minutes in Rhode Island and my luck was returning true to form.

Fat Albert was, I will admit, dressed quite nicely. I say that because heretofore I would have thought that a being with his girth could only be covered by tent canvas. But apparently the Ocean State subscribes to a chain of VERY Big and Tall stores, of which Albert here was most certainly a charter member.

He wore a powder blue button-down shirt with a hunter green pinstripe suit jacket and matching slacks. He wore no necktie, but left his shirt collar open, and who could blame him? I counted at least four chins already, any of which could cut off the air path to his lungs if given the right amount of pressure. And giving mouth-to-mouth resuscitation to Mountain Man here was about as tempting as having unprotected sex with Courtney Love. Or any other member of the fungus family.

As he raised his glass to his mouth, I noticed two gold bracelets dangling from his wrist. Adding that to the diamond pinky ring he had on his left hand, along with a watch that I was sure cost more than my last three cars combined, it soon became apparent how Blond Girl was able to afford her perma-smile.

The only true friend I had made so far was the alcoholic beverage in my highball glass, and even that was rapidly leaving me. I ordered one more. Might as well keep your true friends around as long as possible.

"You're new here, aren't you?"

I turned to my right to see Fat Albert looking at me over Blond Girl's head. His face was a huge smile, and his teeth literally sparkled. I was beginning to feel embarrassed about my fillings.

"Actually, I just got here," I said.

"Yep, I knew it," he said, smiling wider and wagging his finger at me. "I know everybody in town. Locals, vacationers, everybody. And I've never seen you around."

"I'm just down for a little vacation."

I smiled at him modestly. I was afraid if I had something stuck between my teeth, he might move to the other end of the bar.

"Well, don't stand on ceremony here," he said, extending his hand. "Albert Crispin. Good to meet you."

Albert.

Really.

God has a sense of humor.

He shook my hand and gave me a business card. Never to be outdone, I gave him one in turn.

"Samuel Miller," he read. "Private investigator. Really? I'll be damned!"

"Aren't we all," I smiled.

"A private investigator on vacation. You must do pretty well for yourself."

"I also own a restaurant in Philadelphia."

"Well, you do get around, don't you?!" he laughed.

"Keeps me busy. Not to be rude," I said to the blond, extending my hand. "We haven't been introduced."

"Melissa Norman." Her smile was automatic.

"Parking gets worse every summer, Al."

A tall, thin man dressed in a black button-down shirt and black jeans tossed a set of car keys on the bar and turned and smiled at me. If he kept up the smile for any length of time, I would have to put my sunglasses on indoors. Dental coverage must be all-inclusive in Rhode Island. Praise the governor.

"Hi," he said. "My name's Abraham Punditt."

"How do you do," I said. "I assume Botox gives a discount if you come three at a time."

His smile remained on his face, but his eyes betrayed the look of patient confusion.

"Abe here is my personal spiritual advisor," Albert said.

Spiritual advisor.

I looked at Albert's card again.

"What exactly does a lawyer need a spiritual advisor for, Al? Does he tell you which clients to accept on a moral basis?"

Abe and Al both gave a patient laugh. They must be used to dealing with ignorance such as mine on a regular basis. Breeding.

"My relationship with Mr. Crispin extends far beyond his mere professional discourse," stated Abraham. "I work with him to ensure that every step of his life leads upwards to higher moral platitudes."

"Ah," I said.

"Mr. Miller here is a private investigator," said Crispin.

"Really?" said Abraham with a bit too much excitement. "Well you and I seem to be in the same line of work!"

"I was just thinking the same thing," I said as I gestured to the bartender to get me another drink.

"We're both in the business of righting wrongs," continued Punditt. "You right them after they have happened, and I guide people to live lives so they don't occur in the first place."

"Lucky we're both so noble," I said.

Punditt went on as if I hadn't even spoken. "I would love to meet with you sometime and compare work tactics. I think it could be beneficial for us both."

"Should I bring my gun?" I asked.

"It's a date then! Al, what do we have on the agenda for tomorrow? I want to get Mr. Miller out to the house to show him what we do."

Maybe I need to speak louder.

"Without a doubt, without a doubt," smiled Crispin. "Why don't you come out to the house tomorrow afternoon." He wrote an address on a cocktail napkin and handed it to me.

"What do you say, Mr. Miller?" breathed Melissa. Her smile beamed. Her eyes were wide. Her hand rested lightly on my knee. "Will you come out for a visit?"

"Sure," I said. "What the hell."

All three of them smiled in accordance at me.

The collective brightness was blinding.

Maybe I should visit my dentist before tomorrow.

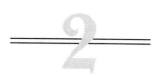

I took the top off the Mustang for the drive home, and just let the humidity blanket me as I drove along Narragansett's Ocean Road. The trees bowed heavily around me and the asphalt ahead of me melted into a hazy blur. The only thing that was anywhere near cool was Keith Richards' rhythm of "Honky Tonk Women" seeping through my stereo.

The houses were set so far back on either side, that as one cruised down, the possibility that Ocean Road was flanked only by driveways and no houses seemed to be very real. These people needed a golf cart to come out and get their mail. Life by the beach.

I pulled into the driveway of the house that we had rented for the month. I could not complain. Two streets up from the beach, the house had two bedrooms, a large living room, a good-sized eat-in kitchen, and the best room: a deck that faced the water. Not too much and not too little. Just right.

I went inside and found my cell phone on the kitchen counter. I had one message. I hit the message button and heard Lil's voice purr over the receiver. "Hey, it's me. Just calling to check in and see how the house is. You're probably at a bar. I'm at the restaurant. I'll be here until eleven, and then I'm leaving from here. Call me when you have a chance."

Nice to be predictable. At least I hung a couple of shirts in the closet before I went out to find a bar.

The message came at two in the afternoon. I looked at my watch. It was five thirty now. I wasn't too late. I dialed the number of the restaurant. Midway through the second ring, Roz's voice cut right in.

"Good afternoon, Four Horsemen Tavern, may I help you?"

"I'd like seventy-six Philly cheesesteaks to go," I said.

Roz's voice dropped about twenty degrees. "Y'know, Samuel, your best trait is that you are a fucking asshole."

"How are you, Roz?" I asked. But Lil's voice was the one that came back on the line.

"She was in a good mood, Sam."

"I could tell."

"We don't even sell Philly cheesesteaks here."

"That's only because I have no say in the menu."

"You have no say in anything, and that's the only reason we make any money."

I could hear the smile on her face.

"How's the house?" she asked.

"Perfect. When are you coming down?"

"Not 'til tomorrow afternoon. We just got word that the forty-second precinct is coming in after their shift tonight. One of the squad just became a daddy – triplets. You know how cops drink. I'll be racing to get out of here by three A.M."

"Been awhile since you ran from the cops," I said.

"Last time I ran from them, I ran right into you."

"Luck's been uphill ever since."

"Who's sitting by the beach, babe? Who's gonna be babysitting a bunch of drunks in a few hours?"

"Good point. You gonna be okay handling an obnoxious crowd?"

"Darling. With whom are you dealing?"

Again I heard that smile.

"I'll end up locking up here. I'll send Roz home about eleven, but I'll keep Jack, Rita, and Todd until close. I should get down to Rhode Island by late afternoon or early evening tomorrow. Are you going to be okay by yourself until then?"

"Oh yeah. I've already made three new friends."

"No doubt. If you get in the way of me doing anything but lying in the sun for the first forty-eight hours I'm there, you will lose a testicle."

"Always a pleasure talking with you."

"I love you." And she hung up.

I turned my cell phone off. The evening was starting to settle in. The days would seem fuller once Lil arrived, but right now there was the nice, peaceful emptiness that comes with summer nights. I put an Aretha Franklin album on, grabbed a bottle of water, and headed out on the deck. A breeze was coming in off the ocean. I put my feet up on the banister and watched the cars move up and down the road, heading home from the beach or going out to dinner.

I put a steak on the grill and let it cook slowly while the night came in off the ocean. I ate my dinner in silence and then cleaned up in the kitchen. A couple of old movies were on TV, which kept me on the couch until about one in the morning.

In preparation for tomorrow, I made sure to brush my teeth twice before going to bed.

I awoke the next morning and searched for a reason to get out of bed. As there was no other occupant sharing the bed with me, that seemed to be reason enough, and by seven thirty, I was out running along Ocean Road, away from Scarborough Beach and toward the center of town. Life is simple, and one of the simple rules of life is to make it to the gym on a regular basis.

I set an easygoing pace, and as I hit the sea wall along Narragansett Beach, a thin sheen of sweat had started at the base of my neck and worked its way down my back. A steady stream of people hit the sea wall at this hour of the morning, and I was greeted with a small throng of early-morning walkers and runners, all of whom carried themselves with that daylong laid-back attitude worn only by people who live by the beach.

Supposedly, back in the day, Narragansett sported quite a casino along this boardwalk, almost all of which was destroyed in a fire. The only remaining structure from that era now is a stone archway flanked on either side by a tower that announces your arrival into the peace and relaxation waiting to engulf you at Narragansett Beach. At seven forty-seven in the morning, I could almost believe that. I wasn't sure that perception would remain later in the day when the beach was populated by tourists trying to squeeze a week's vacation out of hot sand, greasy sunblock, and seven-dollar hot dogs. But what did I know?

I turned around at the Towers and picked up the pace for the run back. By the time I got home, I had run about six miles. My body was covered in a thin layer of sweat, but I wasn't breathing hard. Nice to know I was still in decent shape. I had heard there was some sort of ten-mile road race through Narragansett taking place next week. A ten-mile run for fun. I don't know what kind of an asshole would run that.

I stripped off my clothes as I entered the cottage and jumped in the shower. I put on a clean pair of shorts, and as the only other product of yesterday's five-minute shopping spree at the local Stop and Shop was a dozen eggs, I cooked up four, grabbed a bottle of water, and ate my breakfast on the deck.

By the time I had everything cleaned up, the beach across the street was in full swing with tourist action. I could hear the lifeguard over the loudspeaker admonishing anyone who dared to erect a volleyball net, toss a Frisbee in the water, toss a Frisbee out of the water, or swim out past the designated buoy. Apparently, sitting on the sand was still allowed.

By the time eleven o'clock rolled around, it was time for me to go visit my newfound friends. I was so excited, I put on my very best pair of jeans. I grabbed my sunglasses and headed out to my car. I wondered if Abraham and I would spend hours poolside talking of higher moral platitudes. Maybe Melissa's platitudes were high. I hoped not. I decided I'd spend more time thinking about things I actually knew. That got me just about to the base of the stairs, so I got into the Mustang and pulled out onto the street.

Albert's home was about ten minutes away in a small section of Narragansett known as Harbor Island, which contains some wealthy manors tucked in amongst smaller two- and three-bedroom cottages.

Albert's home wasn't the biggest on the block, but what it lacked in size, it made up for in presence. The basic framework alluded to the fact that at one time it had been a beach cottage, but there had been some formidable improvements. An additional floor had been added, and the two front corners both jutted out in a rounded turret shape. A three-car garage adjoined the left side of the house, but Albert still left his Jaguar outside in the circular driveway, advertising his success to the millions of plaintiffs in need. A balcony came off the window of the right turret, and wove around into a deck that extended along the side, and I would bet my best bottle of whiskey, emptied into a pool in the backyard.

I made the journey up the driveway to the house itself, saying prayers of thanks that I filled up my gas tank yesterday. I parked behind the Jag, and steeled myself for the hours of scintillating discussion that was sure to follow. As I walked up the stairs and knocked on the ornate oak front door, I found it was already partly open.

"Hey Al, do you charge an hourly rate for parking here, or do I have to tip the attendant?"

No answer. Everybody's probably already out at the pool drinking piña coladas.

"Anybody home?" I asked as I pushed the door open and entered the house.

I stepped into the foyer and looked around. To my right was an ornate dining room, and to my left was what looked to be a library or an office. In front of me was a set of stairs leading to the second floor. I stepped into the library and decided to make my way to the back of the house, where I assumed the pool and a scantily clad Melissa Norman awaited.

"Hello?" I called. No answer.

The room beyond the library was a good-sized kitchen. As I walked through, I saw that I won my bet. Through the windows in the kitchen, I saw a huge in-ground swimming pool in the backyard. But no one was there.

I looked to my left into the solarium off the kitchen, and saw that I was mistaken. There was someone here. Lying on the floor of his solarium, two bullet holes in his head, was Albert Crispin.

His smile wasn't half as bright as it was yesterday.

Twenty-two hours in Rhode Island and my luck was right up to par.

The nice thing about having a cell phone is now you can call the local police at a moment's notice and be charged by the minute for doing your civic duty. But as I had now inadvertently stumbled onto a murder scene, I decided to bite the bullet — not literally — and pay the two-dollar charge for the phone call. Better to leave as much undisturbed as possible, and that included the fingerprints of whoever had last used the phone.

To their credit, the police arrived relatively quickly. Apparently, no one was surfing on the wrong wave or anything. Three officers arrived on the scene. Two of them started immediately examining the body and room. The third identified herself as Sergeant Lucille Simon and pulled me back into the library where she could question me in private.

Sergeant Simon had large blue eyes that dominated her small, round face. Her nose and mouth were small, and what makeup she did wear was applied simply and well. Her face had a shiny clean look to it, and her black hair was pulled back in a French braid. When she spoke, she looked directly at me, and the force in her eyes alone could knock you back into the wall.

"Could I see some identification please?"

I gave mine to her.

She looked at my ID and then back at me.

"Ah, a private investigator. And you just happened to stumble across a dead body. Of course."

"Yeah, I know," I smiled. "Not exactly my choice of a way to start off a vacation."

"Vacation," she said as she glanced back at my ID. "Tell me, Mister Miller, is it commonplace in Philadelphia to let yourself into complete strangers' homes?"

"Now that's not fair. I've been a close friend of Mr. Crispin's for almost twenty-four hours."

"You're not funny."

Her distinct lack of a smile let me know she wasn't joking.

"I have a prominent, well-known citizen of this community shot dead in his own home, found by a no-name from Philadelphia. I don't like the situation, I don't like the pretense, and right now, I don't like you. Why don't you tell me what you're doing here. And if I don't like your answers, we can do this down at the station."

"I met Mr. Crispin and his friends yesterday at a bar. He invited me out to his house."

I showed her the cocktail napkin with Al's phone number on it that was in my pocket.

"I got here, the door was open, I let myself in, I found Crispin, and I called you. That's the story. I'm not carrying a gun, I have no powder residue on my hands, and I highly doubt you're going to find any gloves on the premises that I could have used."

"I wouldn't bet on that, Chief," one of the other policemen called out as he came into the library.

He was a short individual with a blond crew cut and very bad sunburn. He looked like he had just graduated high school, never mind the police academy. His mom had probably ironed his uniform for him before he left this morning. He was carrying two plastic bags, which he handed to Lucille.

"Plastic gloves. We found these out back in the garbage. They do have powder residue on them. Thing is, they're very small."

Sergeant Simon looked at them.

"Well, you obviously couldn't fit into these, Mr. Mill—"

"Is everything all right?" Abraham Punditt hurried up the front steps and hurried into the library. He was wearing black slacks, a white button-down shirt, and a grey sweater vest. His wingtips were glamorously polished, and it was all he could do not to scuff them as he moved from one officer to the other with the grace of a Disney animatron. He was so busy demanding answers and asking questions that nobody else was able to speak for a full ten minutes.

Melissa Norman followed in tow, wearing a little more relaxed attire, dressed in a dark blue bikini top and a flowered wrap. Her blond hair had been meticulously styled, and sunglasses were perched atop her head. She smiled when she saw me and then looked confused when she realized there where three people here who had not been invited yesterday.

When Abraham finished his frantic interrogation, he slowly came over to Melissa and stood in front of her.

"I'm afraid – I'm afraid there's some bad news," he said, looking down at the hardwood floor.

We all stood in silence for a minute and a half before Sergeant Simon made her way over to Melissa and quietly led her into the dining room.

"Ohmigod. Ohmigod. Ohmigod."

The sound of Melissa's voice from the next room was made all the more childlike being heard in the vacuous silence. She came back into the room shaking, and sat down on the leather couch in the library and stared at nothing. Abraham had moved himself into the furthest corner in the room and would not look at anyone, but continued to stare at the floor. I looked over at Sergeant Lucille Simon.

"How long are you here on vacation?" she asked.

"I have the cottage rented for four weeks," I replied. "But if this is considered the fun part of Narragansett, Rhode Island, I may not stay through Tuesday."

"I'd appreciate you remaining in the area for some time," she said. "Do you have a phone number where you can be reached?"

I gave her one of my cards.

"The second number is my cell phone number. If I don't pick up, just leave a message. I'll return any call within twenty-four hours."

"Mister Miller, I have a distinguished member of my town dead by murder," she snapped. "You'll come when I call. Until then, if you think of anything at all that could help this investigation, you will be sure to contact me immediately."

I thought about how Sergeant Simon had referred to Crispin as distinguished, prominent, and well-known. Everything except well-respected. That seemed to me to be a good place to start. But this was not my town, this was not my job, and I was not getting paid. So I put on my sunglasses and left through the front door.

Besides, I was sure Abraham would be more help than they needed.

The good news was that despite the morning's events, nothing had deterred my appetite. At least my vitals were still working. I drove to the other end of Route 108 and found a restaurant tucked up on the hill. I went inside and ordered a very rare hamburger with coleslaw and potato salad for sides. The hamburger was good sized and the juice soaked right into the bun. I was impressed. As far as this vacation was going, the burger was the best thing that had happened to me so far.

I ate my lunch and thought about what had transpired. In retrospect, I didn't know much, other than Albert Crispin was dead. Of that I was pretty sure. Lucille Simon was very serious about her job, Melissa Norman wasn't the quickest brain in class, and I still didn't know what the hell Abraham Punditt was. It was actually a source of pride that I didn't understand him.

Anyway, none of this was my problem. I paid my tab and left with every intention of pursuing my vacation. Which explained why as I exited through the door, it was pouring rain outside. I got into my car and figured I'd at least score some points with Lil before she arrived, and drove to the strip mall across the street.

Lil had threatened me with bodily harm if I got in the way of her relaxing during her stay here, but I had known Lil long enough to know that her moods changed quicker than the weather. And sometimes with not as much grace. I went into the Staples in the mall and picked up three reams of computer paper and a couple of printer cartridges. I knew she'd bring her laptop with her, and if she got the mind to get some work done while she was down here, she might as well be prepared. With the rain dictating the direction of my day, I stopped by the bookstore and after wandering aimlessly for twenty minutes, I left with an autobiography of Ray Charles and headed home.

The rain pelted the roof of my car as I drove, and by the time I reached the cottage, the early afternoon sky had been cloaked in premature blackness. A day like this was all right every once in awhile. It forced you to slow down. Although lately, if I slowed down any more, I would lose my pulse.

Lil's Jeep was in the driveway when I pulled in and lights were on inside the house. She'd made better time than she expected. I walked up the staircase on the side and entered through the door to the kitchen, where Lil was unpacking groceries.

"You break any speed records on the way here?"

"You didn't lock the door," she said without looking up from unpacking. "Someone could've walked right in and taken six or even eight eggs."

"I like to keep my thieves honest. Besides, if they broke a window, then I'd have to clean up the glass."

"I'm sure that would've taken up your entire afternoon," she said in an Irish lilt that was as pleasing to hear as her grin was to see.

She turned and gave me the full-wattage smile, and if I had a heart, I'm sure it would have stopped. She was dressed simply in a white halter top, blue jeans, and black boots. Her deep green eyes speared directly into mine, and her long red hair managed to shimmer incandescently, even in the dimly lit cottage.

People who met Lil didn't know what to initially make of her, and once they got to know her, they kept their distance. She was tall and thin, not from dieting, but from regular exercise. She was fiercely intelligent, and had no formal schooling that I ever knew of. But her most formidable asset was her attitude. She garnered command of a room simply by walking through the front door. I'd seen her speak calmly to street thugs, only to kick them to the ground once she got their attention. I'd also seen her fly into a rage at various politicians and corporate reps who happened into the restaurant. Sound and fury, she was the eye of the storm and the storm itself.

God knows why she spends time with me.

She ran her hand back through her hair as she kissed me hello, and the two gold bracelets I gave her a couple Christmases ago jangled down her arm.

"I picked you up some catfish at the market," she said, "and a bottle of Jameson's as well."

She poured me a drink over ice, and poured herself a glass of bourbon neat. She handed me my drink and we went into the living room.

"I don't know why everyone describes you as scary. I think you're sweet."

She smiled at me.

"You tell anyone and I'll kick your fucking ass."

We sat in the dark for a while and listened to the rain.

"Work was even busier than I thought it'd be last night. I didn't get home 'til close to four thirty."

I looked at her.

"You made really good time."

"I only slept for an hour and a half. I didn't feel like putting my vacation off any longer."

The rain drove even harder onto the roof and thunder could be heard in the close distance.

"So," she said, "we have a romantic little cottage across from the beach, and it doesn't look like the rain will let up for hours. What do you propose we do?"

"I just picked up a book on Ray Charles."

"Oh. A book."

She finished her drink, went into the kitchen, and came back with a second. She sat back down on the couch, took off her boots, and put her feet up on the coffee table. She leaned back into the couch and stretched.

"Books can be very stimulating."

"Educational."

Lil stood up, slid out of her jeans and walked over to the stereo. She searched until she found a jazz station and let the music fill up the room. She turned around, took off the halter top and walked back to the couch. Her body was warm and smelled of lilacs as she curled up next to me.

"Still want to read a book?" she whispered as she kissed my cheek.

"No point," I said as I leaned in to kiss her. "It's Ray Charles. It's probably in Braille."

After we were done christening the living room, Lil and I lay entwined on the couch, listening to the storm which was now in full force. Every so often, lightning would flash and light up the whole room for a moment.

Lil was an all-or-nothing girl, and now that she was asleep, she wasn't waking up for a while. I carried her into the bedroom and put her under the covers, making sure to crank up the air conditioner before I shut the door. I went back to the kitchen and finished cleaning up. I made myself a couple corned beef sandwiches and sat at the table by the window. The rain beating against the roof sounded so strong that if it wasn't July, I would've thought it was hail.

I finished my second sandwich and came back to the living room. I had spent the better half of the last month scouring the used CD shops in Philly, looking for an early album of Joan

Osborne. I finally found it in a small shop outside Washington Square. Lil didn't understand why I didn't just order it off the Internet. Half the fun was searching through the shops and witnessing the different histories of music that became entangled with one another as you delved through collection after collection.

I put Joan on softly and read the first four chapters of Ray's autobiography. Then I lay back down on the couch and listened to the storm for another half an hour before I fell asleep myself.

7

I'm sure there are more annoying sounds than your cell phone ringing at four thirty in the morning, but as mine was doing exactly that at precisely that time, I was hard pressed to find one. I disentangled myself from the couch and stumbled out to the kitchen, where I had left it charging on the counter. I pulled up the antenna and answered the phone in my cordial, professional manner.

"Yeah."

"Mister Miller?"

I couldn't quite place the voice.

"Yeah."

"Are you sure?"

That would make it Melissa Norman.

"Pretty sure."

"This is me. I mean Melissa Norman. I met you a couple days ago at a bar with Albert Crispin and Mister Punditt."

"I've seen you once since then, Melissa."

"What? Oh yes. Yesterday. I try not to think about that. I'm sorry to be calling you so late. I mean, early. But – "

She was speaking faster than the Road Runner runs from the Coyote.

"I think I really need your help."

She stopped talking for a moment and I let that sink in.

"I mean, I think I will. They finally let me out of the police station half an hour ago."

"Who's 'they'? You mean Sergeant Simon?"

"Yes, she's one of them. She took me down to the police station right after you left. She and two other policemen have been questioning me since this afternoon. I'm scared, Mister Miller. I think they think I did it. Hurt Albert, I mean. I really need to see you. I don't know what else to do. Could I see you, Mister Miller? Please?"

Twenty-four hours ago I wouldn't have passed up a chance to visit with Melissa Norman. Of course it takes a murder to get her to want to see me.

"Sure, Melissa. I'll see you. Do you want to see me now?"

"Oh no. I need to get cleaned up first. I'm a mess. But I don't think I'll be able to sleep at all. Could I see you at a more decent hour? Maybe nine?"

"Nine would be fine, Melissa. Where would you like to meet?"

"Oh, I don't want to go anywhere that's public. God knows what the media will already be saying. I know you're on vacation, but would it be too much of an imposition to meet you at your place?"

God really does have a sense of humor.

"No imposition at all, Melissa," I said and gave her the address. "Try to calm yourself down. I'll see you soon."

I hung up the phone.

Lil was going to love this.

It was pointless to try to go back to sleep at this point, so I put on a pair of jeans and a T-shirt, and drove up the road to a convenience store and bought a newspaper. Apparently Albert Crispin wasn't as prominent as he thought, as his death only made the front page of the second section of the paper, and below the fold at that. The main front page was reserved for a three-way sex scandal that was occurring in the White House. All Albert had was two bullet holes in the head. How could he compete?

I took the paper back to the cottage and read the overview of Crispin while I sat on the deck. The sun was starting to rise, and gave ample light by which to read. Albert Crispin had led a very accomplished, if not exciting life. The article recounted his educational background and success as a lawyer, but otherwise, it was pretty bland. He hadn't represented anyone famous or notorious, hadn't dated anyone well-known; in fact, he was never married, nor did he have any children. The only reason that seemed to garner him any recognition in the Narragansett community at all was the fact that he donated large sums of money, which seemed to finally come to take shape in the Crispin Recreational Fields, consisting of two soccer fields, a baseball diamond, two basketball courts, and four tennis courts, all given for the use of the good people of Narragansett. Apparently, giving money to the town earned you the right to be called "prestigious" by a police sergeant. Or maybe it was just having a house the size of Wisconsin.

The good news was that the article didn't mention Melissa Norman at all. In fact, it didn't mention anyone at all who seemed like a good candidate to kill Crispin. Even my buddy Abraham was left out with nary a word of his advising Crispin in spiritual matters.

I went back inside and poured myself a tall glass of orange juice. Melissa wouldn't be here for three hours, and Lil wasn't waking up until she was good and ready. I traded my jeans in for a pair of sweatpants, left Lil a note in case she did wake up, and headed out for a morning run.

I ran the same route I ran yesterday, but since I actually knew where I was going this time, I was able to pick up the pace a little. My joints were a little stiff from sleeping on the couch, but about a mile in, my body got into a rhythm and was fine.

I finished my run and walked the beach to cool down, then took a quick shower when I returned. Lil was still sleeping, so I cooked up some eggs, toasted an English muffin, and started the coffee brewing. By the time Melissa was knocking on my door at eight thirty, I was showered, dressed, fed, and wide awake.

I opened the door for her and she looked tentatively around my kitchen, making up her mind about whether she wanted to enter, and then smiled at me and stepped in. She looked very fresh for having been up all night, and her makeup had been applied very carefully. Her hair still looked styled and I was beginning to wonder if it would budge in a hurricane wind. She wore a white blouse, dark skirt, and heels. I led her through the kitchen into the living room. She sat on the couch, placing her hands on her knees. I sat in one of the chairs facing her, trying to look relaxed and attentive.

"Thank you for seeing me on such short notice. I didn't know where to go. Mr. Punditt gave me your number. He suggested I call you."

I didn't remind her that I had given my card to Crispin, not to Punditt. "Was he with you at the police station?"

"No, he was taken down with me, but they let him go a couple of hours later. When I finally got out, I checked my messages and he had called me seven times. He's really a good man. I called him before I called you, and he suggested you'd be able to help me."

She looked up as Lil walked into the living room wearing her silk robe and running her fingers through her hair as she finished waking up.

"Oh, I'm sorry," Melissa said. "I didn't know you had company."

Lil stopped short and looked at Melissa and then looked over at me.

"Neither did I," she said.

"Melissa Norman," I said, "Lillian Cassidy."

"How do you do?" Melissa said.

"It's a pleasure," Lil smiled. "Would you care for some coffee, Melissa?" Lil asked as she walked into the kitchen.

"No thank you," Melissa answered, and looked back at me.

Lil poured herself a cup of coffee, took the newspaper, and went out to the deck.

"I'm really scared, Mister Miller," Melissa said in a voice much more childlike than it had been minutes before. "I don't have anyone to go to."

"Sure you do," I said.

Melissa stared at me.

"Excuse me?"

"Albert Crispin was a prominent lawyer. I don't know how well you knew him, but I'm sure there are plenty of associates of his you could call on for help. I don't know Rhode Island that well, but I'm sure if you look in the Yellow Pages under "Detectives" or "Investigators," you'll find plenty of choices and you can begin consulting with them and see which one would be a good match for you."

Melissa continued to stare at me.

"I'm sorry," she said in a flat tone. "Are you telling me you're not going to help me?"

Any trace of a childish tone had left her voice.

"Yeah, that's about it."

Melissa's face turned red.

"You piece of shit," she spat.

She grabbed her purse, and in as dignified a manner as she could in her three-inch heels, stormed out through the kitchen, slamming the door behind her.

Lil came in off the deck and looked at me.

"You're making friends fast, babe."

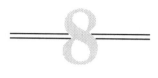

I cut myself half a cantaloupe and joined Lil out on the deck, where I proceeded to explain to her the events that had precipitated Melissa's stately exit from our vacation cottage. When I reached any portion of the story that contained Abraham Punditt, she asked me to repeat that part slowly to make sure she had understood me correctly. Satisfied that he was not representative of Rhode Island's typical population, she affirmed that we could remain in Narragansett for the rest of our vacation.

"What I don't understand," Lil said as she spooned off a bite of my cantaloupe, "is why you're not going to help her."

"I'm on vacation."

"Yes, but I thought the whole reason you left the U.S. Marshals was so you could work with people on a more direct level. She certainly seems like she could use some help."

"The whole reason I left the Marshals was because I didn't like the way they did things."

"That's right. And you worked as a marshal for how long?"

"Three days."

"More than enough time to learn the ins and outs of an operation and become properly fed up and disgusted."

"I'm a quick study."

"As I recall, you were pretty successful during your three days. You found that senator's missing daughter in record time, and she ended up where? Nevada?"

"Just a matter of asking the right people the right questions."

"You also worked fifty-one hours straight to get the job done."

I smiled. "You've been talking with Everett too much."

"He speaks very highly of you."

I was quiet.

"I should have done more."

Lil kissed my hand. "Not your fault her father was an asshole."

"Easy to say."

"And it's a wondrous coincidence that the *Washington Post* received an anonymous packet of photos four months later depicting a certain senator engaging in a variety of scandalous acts."

I smiled. "Took me awhile to dig up all those photos."

"Pretty much destroyed his career."

"I had some free time."

The sun was up, shining with a brightness that promised a reversal of yesterday's weather.

Lil stood up, leaned over, and kissed me on the mouth. "You're a good man, Samuel. Now I am going to the beach. Why don't we plan on having dinner together around eight?"

"Sounds good," I said, carrying my empty bowl to the sink. "It's my turn to cook, so enjoy yourself. Be careful you don't get any funny-looking tan lines."

Lil looked over her shoulder as she walked to her bedroom.

"I don't plan on having any tan lines."

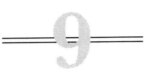

If Lil said we'd be eating at eight, that meant she'd be staying at the beach until seven fifty-nine. With an entire day to do a whole lot of nothing, I took the top off the Mustang, cranked up the radio, and set out to cruise around Narragansett. I headed down into the center of town back the way I had run this morning. The beach traffic was in full swing, and the Sea Wall was littered with tourists carrying beach chairs, blankets, and coolers toward the Mecca of sand and surf that awaited them.

Past the Towers on the left was a town green, and as I drove by I could see preparations being made for some sort of outside concert. Every member of the band was already dressed in full black tuxedos, and they were all sweltering profusely in the heat as they lugged their instruments toward the gazebo where they would play.

I drove extra slowly around the beach area, but surprisingly, no college girls jumped off the walkway into my car asking to be whisked away to fulfill all their private fantasies. Actually, even the moms didn't give me a second look when I was stopped at a red light. With that many strikes against me this early in the day, I turned left at the light and drove back south on 108 toward Galilee. I wasn't much of a beachgoer anyway.

Down the southern tip of Route 108 or Point Judith Road as it's otherwise known, is an access road that leads down to the section of Narragansett known as Galilee. I had read an article describing this section of town, but the article did not do Galilee justice.

Galilee was an old-fashioned fishing village, and it looked as if time had stopped moving here decades ago. Across from the access road were all the docks, and the boats were the old-fashioned kind, complete with masts, sails, and multi-pronged steering wheels. I was willing to bet at least one captain had an anchor on his arm. Probably even a parrot named Polly.

I parked the car on the street and walked down the road. Next to the docks was the landing for the Block Island Ferry. The tourists waiting for its arrival were strewn about in something resembling a line. Suitcases were piled, bicycles were locked, hats and sunblock were being purchased by the truckload, and nine out of ten people were eating at least two ice cream sandwiches. A postcard shot.

Walking away from the landing, you were consumed by old working man's New England. Storefronts and restaurants advertised on plain white placard signs. Coupons for half off your dinner were handed out on the street on photocopied papers. No neon lights flashed in your face. No announcements blared over an intercom. The smell of the seaport was obviously present, but in this setting was quietly reassuring.

The tourists were easy to pick out: people dressed in T-shirts and shorts taking pictures of their families, buying souvenirs, and complaining about the price of the food. But the working people were easy to pick out as well: tough-looking people older than they should be. People carrying heavy loads from the boats to the markets. People who addressed each other with a simple nod or wave. They did not have time to socialize. Tomorrow might not be as profitable as today. These were good people.

I found a restaurant on the second floor of one of the storefronts and climbed the wooden steps up to the deck. There were about eight tables scattered around the deck, only two of which were occupied. An open sliding glass door led inside to the bar, which was populated less than outside.

I sat down at the bar and the bartender came over to take my order. She wore a white T-shirt and blue jeans. We probably shopped at the same place. She had a hard tanned face and long dirty blond hair. I ordered a bloody mary. She took my order. I smiled at her. She walked away. Up to par. I looked up and down at the empty seats surrounding the bar, and lied to my ego, saying she undoubtedly had many more important things to be doing than talk to me. I looked to my right and she was leaning against the cash register, smoking a cigarette and watching *The Price is Right* on one of the other TVs. I needed to work on my smile.

I studied the menu and decided on the fisherman's stew. The waitress came back to take my order. I smiled at her again. She smiled back. Progress. The Little League World Series was on the TV overhead and Bad Company played out from the jukebox. Oh well, life couldn't be perfect.

I swiveled in my chair and stared out the sliding glass door while I sipped my bloody mary. The boats moved slowly in and out of the harbor. Nobody seemed rushed. I could get used to this pace.

My cell phone rang. I looked at the caller ID as I raised the antenna and answered it.

"Everett."

"What are you up to, my friend?"

"Playing house."

"No doubt. I was successful in commandeering information regarding Abraham Punditt."

Everett spoke like a telemarketer trying to sell you fiscal stability through global economy mutual funds.

"How long did Lil wait before calling you?"

"She said she had just lain down her blanket and arranged her beach chair to allow for maximum tannage of her entire body."

"'Maximum tannage'?"

"Her words. So your man Punditt has an office in East Greenwich, Rhode Island, where I believe he is some sort of mail order monk."

"Spiritual advisor."

"That's it. Apparently rents out his heavenly guidance to the highest bidder. But the interesting facets to this gentleman do not stop there."

"Do tell."

"Well, up until six years ago, Abraham Punditt didn't even exist. Back in 1998, he was one Francis Mortimer Boulet, living in Attleboro, Massachusetts."

"If I had a name like Francis Mortimer, I'd probably change it too."

"To Abraham Punditt?"

"Good point."

"Francis Mortimer was involved in some sort of off-track betting operation. I don't know yet how deep he was, if he was running the operation, making payments, arranging drop-offs, but that's not important. Francis was picked up by the local police in Attleboro; arresting officer, Lawrence Oakes.

Once he turned over a couple names Oakes wanted to hear, he left Attleboro rather quickly and hid out in a seminary in Connecticut for a year. Then he changed his name to Punditt, moved to Rhode Island, and began massaging the souls of the Ocean State's famous."

"You got all this in half an hour?"

"It's called a computer with access. So I'm thinking Nicole and I are coming down tomorrow, you and I can wander over to East Greenwich and see what's what."

"What's what? What's nothing, Everett. There's nothing to see. He's got an office in East Greenwich. Good for him. I don't care. I could give a shit that he used to live in Massachusetts. It's too bad that a man was shot, but it's not my problem. I'm sure the police here are competent, and they'll figure something out."

I took my bloody mary out on the deck and sat down in one of the chairs.

"Lil said a young woman came to you seeking help in this matter."

"And I sent her in the right direction to get proper help. Everett, I am on vacation. I am not working. Which of those concepts do you not understand?"

"Nicole and I should arrive tomorrow morning around eleven. Why don't we table this discussion until later in the day? We can resume talks after we're all properly settled in."

"Like fuck," I said and hung up.

I picked up my half-empty glass and returned to the bar. I had enjoyed my conversation with the bartender better than the one I just finished with Everett. My stew was waiting for me when I sat back down. The bowl was huge and filled to the brim. Galilee didn't skimp on the serving size. I had scallops, shrimp, mussels, and clams all resting in a thick red sauce over a pile of linguine.

Everett and I met during my three-day stint with the U.S. Marshals. He was a Secret Service agent at the time. He has since retired, but he and his wife Nicole have put Everett's MBA to good use, making solid investments over the past years, our restaurant being one of them. Everett is a workaholic perfectionist whose mind never shuts down. He can find, analyze, and store information in inhuman quantities. I, on the other hand, have trouble remembering my Zip Code. Sharing my vacation with him was going to be a huge pain in the ass.

The bartender came back over to see if I wanted another drink. I declined.

"What's your name?" I asked.

"Rebecca," she replied.

"Pleased to meet you, Rebecca," I said extending my hand. "My name's Samuel Miller."

For once, she smiled for real. It was about time.

"Well, Rebecca, I have the entire day to wander around. Any suggestions?"

"There's an art festival two towns over in Wickford. It's going on all week long. The work is actually pretty good – I don't know if you're into that type of stuff."

The only alternative I could think of was remaining at the bar, and I had already done that the past two days. Time for something different. I ate my lunch, got directions from Rebecca, thanked her, and paid my bill. Then I headed for Wickford.

Wickford, Rhode Island is the type of town that is used as a cover for *Yankee* magazine. It's a tiny little hamlet, for lack of a better word, that is hidden right off of scenic Route 1A. The houses are the classic style Victorians built amongst the docks leading out to the harbor. The main street winds through the center of town and showcases the pharmacy, the grocery store, the clock shop, the bookstore, the women's clothing shop, the local bank, and the bakery, all of the mom-and-pop variety. And for this week, the main street was shut down and overrun by artists all setting up their tents and plying their wares to the masses who wandered through.

The crowd was large but tame. There were no overbearing sounds or smells that accompanied the event. This was not a carnival atmosphere. This was a gathering of artists who wanted to display and compare their work. Of course, if you wanted to toss a couple of bucks their way, they weren't going to spit on you either.

I wandered through the various tents, partaking of the festivities. There were paintings, photographs, and etchings of all sizes, some matted and framed, some still in progress. I didn't claim to be any type of art aficionado, but I knew what I liked and what I didn't. After about fifteen minutes, I was sick of paintings of tall-masted boats and psychedelic fish. I had seen starfish in a plethora of various positions, which — being acquainted with the general shape of a starfish — I really hadn't thought possible, and I had viewed about sixteen hundred different paintings of lighthouses. Sadly, there was more variety with the starfish.

I was admiring a black-and-white photo of a couple walking on the beach in the rain when I looked up to see none other than Melissa Norman walking out of the corner pharmacy straight toward me. She had changed into a pair of khaki shorts and a black T-shirt, and was wearing a pair of Nike running shoes. Her legs weren't as good as I remembered them being, but I was probably just jaded from our earlier meeting.

"Glad to see you looking more relaxed than you were this morning," I said as she browsed through the paintings in the neighboring tent.

She looked over at me. She was wearing large, rounded sunglasses with thick frames.

"Excuse me?" Her voice had evolved from her childlike tone into more of a snarl.

She returned her attention to the tent and began idly flipping through the pages of the artist's collection.

"Look, I hope I wasn't too short earlier. If you want to talk and get anything off your chest, I'd be more than happy to join you for a cup of coffee."

She turned toward me and removed her sunglasses, adding a glare to her snarl.

"Hey bud, take one good look at my ass and be on your way."

"Pardon me?"

"Get a cup of coffee. That one's old pal. Time to come up with some new material."

She closed the painter's collection book and turned and stormed off. I noticed a red rose tattoo on her left ankle as she walked away. I also noticed that her ass wasn't half as nice as it had seemed a couple days ago at the bar. Must be the lighting.

Trying not to let Melissa's rejection threaten my manhood, I took another hour to peruse the rest of the items in the art festival. I did find one photo of a wolf staring out of a snow-covered thicket of trees. I would have picked it up, but where the hell was I going to put it? I took the photographer's card and promised to visit his Web site to see his other wildlife photos. I figured Lil would work the computer for me.

I took the scenic route back home, driving along the shore wherever I could, and made one stop at the market for dinner. By seven thirty, I was in the kitchen with a pot of mussels and linguine simmering on the stove, a salmon steak slowly cooking in the oven, and two catfish fillets cooking in a Creole sauce I had discovered on a visit to New Orleans. I even had the red beans and rice as a side dish.

Lil came up the back deck, brushing the sand off her and placing her towel and chair over in the corner. She opened the sliding glass door and stepped through into the living room.

"Who are we listening to?" she asked as she came into the kitchen.

"AC/DC."

"Well, isn't that romantic."

"Wait'll I light the candles."

Lil was full of color as well as sand from her day at the beach, and headed for the shower to clean up before dinner. I set the table in the meantime while the dinner finished cooking. Lil reappeared twenty minutes later wearing a pair of cutoff shorts and a white button-down shirt that I could've sworn used to be mine. She filled a pitcher with ice water for the two of us, grabbed some glasses, turned off the stereo, and joined me at the table.

The salmon was a nice pink color, and the red beans and rice were perfect for the hot weather. My catfish was fine. We sat down to eat in one of those relaxed summer nights where there was no pressure for tomorrow to arrive.

"How was your day at the beach?"

"I have been waiting for this vacation for a long time. I read, I relaxed, I swam, I people-watched. It was nice to have twenty-four hours of no responsibilities."

"What do you plan on doing tomorrow?"

"Extend those twenty-four hours to forty-eight. Did Everett call you?"

You had to admire the fact that she didn't hide anything.

"Probably twenty seconds after he hung up with you. And of course he had the entire family history of Abraham Punditt."

"How good for the two of you. And what do you two plan to do with this information?"

She patted her lips with her napkin and looked at me in earnest. Her face did not betray a hint of amusement, but her eyes danced with joy.

"I do believe I just heard you say how much you had been looking forward to this vacation."

"Yes. You did."

"And also how you enjoyed having no responsibilities while you were here."

"Right again."

"Well, babe, where exactly does my vacation fit into all this?"

"Don't be silly. You know how easily Everett gets bored. This will give him something to do while he's down here."

"Good for him. I'll set him up at the local library and I'll loan him my gun. He can work on this 'til his heart's content."

"You know very well you will not. Neither of you would allow the other to go into a situation alone where you could get hurt."

"Lil, I don't have a case. There's no client. No retainer. No paycheck."

"What about Little Miss Nipple who visited you this morning?"

"I didn't know you knew her Christian name. Actually, I saw her this afternoon, and based on her reaction, I don't think I really merit on her top ten list anymore."

"There's a surprise."

"Only been here three days."

"Took awhile, didn't it."

We finished our dinner, cleaned off the plates, and filled an oversized bowl with the mussels and linguine. I found two small plates and some silverware, and we went out onto the deck. Lil had brought some tourist pamphlets out with her, and she leafed through them while we finished our meal. She planned a day to visit Newport, and wanted to look into purchasing tickets to the Arts Center in Providence, which was hosting a symphony for three weeks.

I put my feet up on the railing, drank some water, and listened to Lil describe the sights she had seen at the beach. Sometimes I just loved listening to her talk. Surprisingly, I had never heard her say the same about me.

We came back inside and cleaned up the kitchen. After enjoying our time on the deck, Lil closed all the windows and turned on the air conditioning. We rarely watched TV, but Lil flipped around until she found a station showing *Rocky*, and we curled up on the couch together and watched the movie. Like she said, it was nice being on vacation and having no responsibilities. We watched the movie from start to finish, and when it was over, we went into her bedroom and went to sleep.

Lil had called ahead from Philly, found a suitable gym for her stay in South County, and had already enlisted the services of a personal trainer. Her first session was at nine A.M., so at eight thirty she was up and out the door. As we had agreed that one of the ways to ensure I kept breathing successfully on my own was not to spend every waking minute together while we were on vacation, I looked through the Yellow Pages and found what looked to be a reputable gym as well. Thus, a little after nine o'clock, I was out the door myself in pursuit of improving my health, or at least watching others in spandex improve theirs.

I found the health club easily enough, and parked and went inside. The receptionist greeted me with a cheery smile and informed me of the day-by-day charges. I paid for two weeks up front. If it was paid for, I would use it. If I only paid for the day, there was always the chance I would come up with some excuse tomorrow and never return.

The gym was nice and open and clean. A block of cardio machines lined the right wall, free weights engulfed the far corner, and two circuits filled up the middle. It was always refreshing to hear the intermittent clanging of the metal weights. It reminded you that you were indeed in a gym, and not a fitness center with people who considered sitting in a sauna and reading the stock reports working out.

I spent half an hour working my shoulders, and another half an hour working my abs. I also gave seven minutes over the course of the hour to contemplating why spandex companies didn't have a cutoff point for sizes they were willing to sell. I used one of the showers in the locker room, and by the time I left, it was almost eleven. I stopped by a Dunkin' Donuts, bought two breakfast sandwiches, and went back to the cottage.

Lil was already getting ready for the beach when I returned, which basically consisted of deciding which bathing suit would be appropriate to wear today. She had settled on a white bikini, which looked to be more string than anything else, and was finishing packing her beach bag when I walked in through the kitchen.

"Did you find a gym?" she called in from the deck.

"Yes. How was your trainer?"

"Woman knows what she's doing. I was surprised I could walk up the stairs when I was done. I'm heading over to the beach. Would you care to join me?"

"Let's see," I said. "Spend time at the beach in the company of you, or stay here and stare at the walls. Tough choice."

"Wouldn't do you any good. I have all the porn blocked on my computer anyway."

"Then I'll just have to stare at you."

I changed into a pair of swimming trunks and a short-sleeved shirt I could leave unbuttoned. Lil was sunning herself on the deck when I came back into the living room. I left a note on the kitchen table for Nicole and Everett when they arrived, picked up my sunglasses and Lil's bag, and we left.

The beach was two streets down from our cottage, so we were able to walk there in about ten minutes. We crossed the parking lot, walked onto the beach, and Lil designated a spot for us on the dry sand a ways up from the water. She lay down her beach towel, opened her beach chair — which probably could fit in her purse — and warned me if I interrupted her sunbathing, various parts of my anatomy would be cast out to sea.

I sat down on my beach towel and took in the sights and listened to the surf. There were some good-sized waves, and the lifeguards kept blowing their whistles when someone swam out too far. I watched the people walking up and down the beach for a while, and then went into the ocean and rode the waves for about half an hour. When I came out of the water, Lil was awake and reading a book. She had been alternating between two books, a romance novel and a psychology book by Carl Jung. Luckily for me, she had notes scribbled in the margins of both.

"I packed some food if you're hungry," she said.

I pulled a turkey sandwich and some grapes out of her bag for my lunch. I was hungry. The meal didn't last long.

"Want to go for a walk, Lil?"

"Sure."

She pulled on a large hat she had stowed in her bag, got up, smiled at me, and took my hand. If I had emotions, I would have been extremely pleased. We walked along the water down to the end of the beach. There was an old stone foundation of what appeared to be farmhouse at the end, and we sat at the edge of the water and let the ocean ebb and flow around us. We stayed there for a little bit enjoying the noontime sun and the ocean breeze.

"Want to stay a couple more hours and then go home?" she asked.

"Sounds good."

She leaned in and kissed me on the cheek.

"I'm glad we're here, Samuel."

"Me too."

We got up and took our time walking back to our part of the beach. We passed swimmers and boogie boarders, kids in diapers playing in the sand, and kids in from college playing with each other. We returned to our blankets, but I grew restless very quickly and jumped back in the water for a while. When I came out, Lil had decided she had had enough, so we packed up and started back toward the cottage.

"Lot of people here," Lil said as she handed me her beach chair.

"I noticed."

"I saw you noticing. Perhaps on our walk back you can explain to me when you became so fascinated with women's volleyball."

There was no good answer to that.

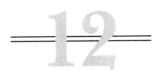

It was mid-afternoon when Lil and I returned to the cottage, and Everett's car was parked in the driveway. He was sitting on the deck and waved to us as we walked up the street. We climbed the stairs and Lil greeted him with a kiss as I piled her beach equipment in the corner. Everett stood up and shook my hand when I turned around. He was dressed in a pink polo shirt and khakis, and his obsidian-colored skin almost shimmered as it reflected the sunlight from the sky. His hair was cropped close to his head and was speckled with grey.

"'Bout time you showed up," I said. "Where's Nicole?"

"Inside unpacking. She's been working straight out and was more exhausted than she realized. The first thing she did when we arrived was take a nap. I think I heard her moving around, so she probably just woke up."

Everett had a stack of newspapers on the table before him, including *The Wall Street Journal*, *The Philadelphia Inquirer*, two Virginian papers I didn't recognize, *The Boston Globe*, and *The Providence Journal*.

"Glad to see you've just been loafing since you got here," I said, motioning toward the table.

"I like to stay apprised of current events that are transpiring in the vicinity," he said. His voice had the tone of a baritone sax and emanated from somewhere deep in his stomach. "You know that."

"Yeah, I know that. Jesus Christ."

Lil had wandered inside, and reappeared with a tray of glasses filled with iced tea. She placed them on the table, being sure not to get any water rings on any of Everett's papers.

"I thought these might be needed," she said.

"Fluids are good," I said, and took a glass, raising it in Everett's direction. Lil made herself comfortable in one of the deck chairs, and I leaned against the railing and faced the table.

Lil apprised Everett of the various profits the restaurant had been making, and Everett enlightened her with a number of stock market insights he had accumulated over the last few days. After a brief foray into Marketing 101 courtesy of Everett Jones, the conversation turned to the menu at the Four Horsemen Tavern, and Everett and Lil entered into an in-depth discussion on additions and specials that should make their way onto our menu. I myself remained stoically quiet throughout all of this. Nobody seemed to mind.

While Everett and Lil plunged into the dessert menu, I gathered up the glasses and went into the kitchen to get a second round. I was a bartender longer than anything else, and some habits die hard. Nicole greeted me in the kitchen as she came out from her bedroom.

"I thought I heard voices out here."

"If you're hearing voices, sweetie," I said, "it's only because you've been listening to Everett for too long and he's got you reciting his mantras in his head."

"For God's sake, Sam, he's not that bad."

"No, but I think a small part of him would love to host a self-help show on cable."

She smiled as I bent down to kiss her cheek.

"Only if people agreed to do things exactly his way."

"There you go, Oprah."

She laughed. Nicole was five feet tall when she wore heels. Her skin was a couple shades lighter than Everett, and her blue eyes were irrepressible. She had a full smile which she showed off often, and was dressed simply in white shorts and a blue T-shirt.

"I think you've gotten taller," I said as I added a fourth glass of iced tea.

"Be careful, Sam. I don't think Lil would argue much if I kicked you in the balls."

"No, she'd probably help hold me down."

Once everyone was sitting out on the deck, we looked ahead to the opportunity for dinner. Lil had already scouted the area and found a restaurant she wanted to try called The Pebble Courtyard.

"Pebble Courtyard," she said, looking at me. "Now isn't that a nice name?"

Lil was forever reminding me that choosing "Four Horsemen" as a name for our restaurant had not been, in her estimation, the brightest point of my life. I tried once to explain to her that the name "Four Horsemen" was representative of the fact that the tavern was owned by Nicole, Everett, her, and me. She responded by saying that she didn't think having Death and Pestilence as fifty percent of a marketing ploy was good business sense for an eating establishment.

Lil found the phone number for The Pebble Courtyard, called and made reservations. Nicole found a baseball game on the radio, and with our dinner plans taken care of, we sat around and enjoyed the sun and listened to the game, and then one by one got cleaned up and ready for a night out.

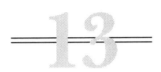

The Pebble Courtyard was a small restaurant facing the ocean. The inside was stately and elegant but not too showy. That boded well. I was a firm believer of the theory that the more expensive the meal, the smaller the portion. Our hostess seated us in the corner at a table for four. The tablecloth was white, the crystal was real, and the view was everything it should be. Some things are almost perfect.

I held Lil's chair for her as she sat. I was dressed simply in a silk button-down shirt, grey cuffed pants, and black belt and shoes. Lil wore her hair back in a headband and was stunning in a straightforward black cocktail dress that I thought was incredibly tame by her standards until I saw the amount of leg that flashed as she took her seat.

"Underwear?" I leaned in to her.

"Heavens no," she smiled.

Everett, being Everett, was dressed in attire that would be appropriate in the event a funeral, wedding, or presidential inauguration broke out while we were in the middle of our dinner. Crisp blue shirt, red tie, black vest, black slacks, black jacket, and polished wingtips.

"You iron your socks?" I asked after he and Nicole were seated.

"Buy them new each time I go out," he said, reaching for the wine list.

He wasn't joking.

"Everett dresses in order to remind himself of the professional presence he wishes to assume for every facet of his life," Nicole smiled. "At least that's my professional opinion."

Nicole was looking quite professional herself in a ruffled red skirt, matching jacket, low-cut black blouse, and heels. She wore a silver heart-shaped pendant on a chain around her neck.

"And what presence are you trying to establish?"

"Sexy as hell, Samuel. I would think that would be obvious."

"Of course."

The waitress was dressed in an elegant white blouse and jeans, and had long brown hair pulled up in a bun. She was fresh out of college, and told us of her plans to travel as she took our drink orders. As rule number seventeen in life is to always forge a good rapport with your waitress, we did, and she arrived moments later with our drinks. No waiting time. It's a good rule.

I had my Jameson's and Lil had her bourbon, and Nicole and Everett shared a bottle of cabernet I could not pronounce. Our appetites properly stimulated and our evening begun, we looked over the menu. We decided to order a tableful of appetizers and split them all among the four of us. We placed our order and settled into our night.

The conversation drifted from Nicole and Everett's new investments to the restaurant in Philly to first impressions of Rhode Island to plans for our vacation. Our food arrived and we picked at it and spoke of movies and music and books. We ordered another round of drinks and told stories of past and present, both shared and individual.

Our memories spent and our stomachs full, we settled back as the house band for the night came out. The band was called "On the Move" and consisted of a drummer, guitarist, bassist, saxophonist, and keyboardist. The drummer did the majority of the singing, but each of the other members of the ensemble took their turn singing a song or two over the course of the first set. The band began their set by launching into Stevie Ray Vaughn, followed by Van Morrison. They played a couple old-school blues covers, two back-to-back Billy Joel songs, and copped a ferocious rendition of The Rolling Stones. They were good, but the most impressive part was the fact that the drummer could sing and play the drums while simultaneously drinking a beer and smoking a cigarette. You can't teach talent like that.

They closed out their first set with a ballad by Bob Dylan, and the four of us being the elegant people we are stepped to the center of the dance floor to enjoy the song. I loved dancing with Lil. She had a natural rhythm to her that made her at home no matter the situation. But when she danced, the music seemed to come up from the floor and take form in her body. She became the rhythm and melted right into the music. Or maybe the music melted right into her.

The band finished their last song and took a break. Everett and I went back to the table while the girls went outside to have a cigarette. Our waitress returned and we ordered another round of drinks.

"Nicole looks great," I said to Everett.

"Yeah, she's very happy. She's meeting with a lot of success at her job. Praise from the higher-ups, articles in the paper, local commendations, the works. She's the most requested shrink on the force."

"You almost say that with resignation."

The waitress returned with our drinks. She gave the two of us a smile that lingered well after she walked away. Inspiring.

"Don't get me wrong, Sam. I would never get in the way of her happiness. But there's a part of me that gets bothered with her success and independence. I know it's wrong, and I know it's selfish, but a part of me wants her to be dependent on me."

"Because as long as she needs you, she'll stay with you forever and ever?"

Everett looked me straight in the eye and grinned.

"Sounds stupid when you say it out loud, doesn't it?"

"A relationship built on dependence will develop into contempt," I said. "She's with you now because she wants to be. If she's independent, she has that choice. Be happy she chooses you. If she was with you because she had to be or was dependent on you, guaranteed she'd start to resent you real quick."

Everett stared at me with a flat gaze.

"My fucking word. That's not bad for a man who should register his sideburns as lethal weapons. You banging a shrink?"

"'Dear Abby' is printed right next to the comics."

We clinked our glasses.

Nicole returned to the table, gave Everett a kiss on the cheek, and he handed her a new glass of wine.

"Where's Lil?" I asked.

Nicole smiled to herself and shook her head slightly. Behind her, the band members took their places once again, and Lil was standing up next to the guitarist.

"We've got a special treat for you tonight, ladies and gentlemen," the drummer said into his microphone. "Our newly acquired friend Lillian here is going to help us out on this next song."

The guitarist had moved his microphone stand out so that Lil was standing in the center of the band. The band started again and the music to "Son of a Preacher Man" struck up behind her. Lil's voice smoldered out of her, and by the third stanza, the entire restaurant was entranced by her voice. She closed her eyes and her body swayed with the music. Her voice had a gravelly quality to it that didn't stand apart from the music but held hands with it and became entrenched with the other sounds. Not bad at all.

She and the band finished and a roar of applause followed. Lil simply smiled and walked back to our table.

"Nice job, babe," I said.

"Just a little better than the godforsaken music you usually bring home."

"I see a duet with you and Steven Tyler in the near future."

"My ass."

"Or that."

We finished our drinks and paid our tab. The girls decided they wanted to go dancing, so I tossed Lil the keys to the Mustang, and she and Nicole headed out to explore the dance clubs in Providence. That left me to ride with Everett, and we decided to explore another restaurant in town.

There was a strip of road in Narragansett that catered to the eating and drinking crowd, where you could find various levels of establishments. Given that I was with Everett and strengthened by the fact that he was driving pretty much mandated that our next stop would be as upscale as our last, if not more so.

True to form, the next stop we made held three separate dining areas, a cigar lounge, an eight-page menu, and an entire wait staff clothed in vests and ties. I swear he researched the area before he arrived and made a list of any restaurant that accommodated you with valet parking.

We took two seats at the bar in the cigar lounge. The dinner crowd had died out and the late-night crowd had not arrived yet, so we pretty much had the room to ourselves. Everett placed our drink orders and I got as comfortable as I could in my wooden straight high-backed chair. I was not that successful.

"Your girl can sing."

"Her name is Lil, Everett."

He chuckled. "It never fails to astonish me how a scrapper like yourself can be so politically correct at times."

"Simple wants, simple pleasures."

I could smell his Sambuca.

"I don't know how you can drink that shit."

"It's relaxing."

"It's toothpaste."

"At least my tastes vary. What have you partaken tonight besides Irish whiskey?"

"C'mon. I had a bloody mary yesterday."

"Speaking of yesterday, we have yet to resume our conversation about why we're not helping this young lady who seems to be in growing peril."

"Drop it already, Everett," I said. "It's getting old."

"I would think you would embrace the opportunity to aid this woman simply out of the intrinsic value it would have on your conscience."

I stared at him for a full minute.

"Do you honestly talk like that or are you just fucking with my head?"

"I believe the proper phrase is 'engaging in fuckery.'"

Even I laughed at that.

"Everett, aside from the fact that my ego is not big enough to believe that I am the only person capable of helping this woman, and the other aforementioned fact that I am indeed on vacation, I don't believe Miss Norman wants my help anymore."

I recounted the scene from the art festival yesterday for him. After a while, even Everett started to realize this was a losing battle and backed off. We spent the next hour and a half enjoying pleasant silences peppered with bits of conversation as we watched random sports highlights on the TV overhead. We paid our tab and decided it was time to go home, so we climbed back into Everett's car and drove back to the cottage. Everett pulled all the way in to the end of the driveway up by Lil's Jeep. We got out of the car and walked up the side stairs to the entrance by the kitchen.

Waiting for us at the top of the stairs, sprawled out on her back, was the dead body of Miss Melissa Norman. The floodlight over the door cast an eerie glow over her pasty face. Everett bent down to examine her body. Her throat had been slit open. The wound was deep and dried with blood. There were rope burns on her wrists. He closed her wide empty eyes and looked up at me.

"I think you're involved in this now, my friend. Whether you're on vacation or not."

The Narragansett police station is located right next to the Narragansett library. I refrained from making any jokes as Everett and I walked in, but I figured the location was either really good karma or a cruel, cruel joke. The building also housed the Narragansett fire department, and from the outside almost looked like a very small apartment complex.

Everett and I were escorted by two uniformed officers into a small conference room with a table and four chairs. Once we were inside, the officers closed the door and stood outside. Everett and I sat down and stared at each of the four walls. After a short discussion, we agreed that each of the walls was equally unattractive and the room as a whole could use some sprucing up, perhaps in a tropical Caribbean theme.

About twenty minutes into our wait, the door opened again, and Sergeant Lucille Simon made her entrance. She was wearing running sneakers, and was dressed in a pair of grey sweatpants, a white T-shirt, and a jean jacket. Her hair looked as if it had been pulled back hastily into a ponytail, and she wore no makeup. Her expression had not grown happier since our last encounter.

"I hope we didn't interrupt a date," I said as she sat down across from us.

"You are pretty goddamned arrogant for such a skinny little fuck," she snapped.

"My girlfriend says the exact same thing. Lucille, I'd like you to meet my friend Mister Everett Jones."

"How do you do," Everett said, standing and extending his hand.

"Sit the fuck down."

"She likes you," I said.

"And you shut your damn mouth." Lucille slammed her hands down on the table as she sat down. "Two homicides in my town since you've arrived, you piece of shit. The second one literally on your doorstep." She flung the police report at me. "I want to know the connection. I want to know now." I honestly thought she was going to lunge across the table at me. A small part of me wondered if I would enjoy it.

I took a moment to look through the police report. The script was brief, and four out of the five pages contained only photographs of the late Melissa Norman. I passed the report over to Everett, folded my hands on the table, and looked directly at the sergeant.

"Sergeant Simon, all joking aside, I don't like this any more than you do. For reasons unbeknownst to me, I am being pulled into something I have no desire to be a part of. But first and foremost, I did not kill that young woman. And I have an alibi and witnesses which can account for that. Why don't you ask us what you want, and then send us home."

"When was the last time you saw Miss Norman?"

"Yesterday morning."

"What were the circumstances?"

"She came to me seeking my professional services. I declined to aid her and tried to help her pursue her other options."

Everett glanced up from the report. I didn't look at him.

"That would seem to be a somewhat unprofitable stand for a private investigator to take."

I smiled. "I didn't think my services would be in her best interests."

"Meaning?"

"Meaning I thought she was annoying as hell."

She paused, as if trying to decide what direction to take next.

"You seem to be repetitive in that behavior Mister Miller. I did some research on you. Three days could be a record for tenure as a U.S. Marshal, especially one of your caliber. As I understand, you found a missing person in less than three days. And a daughter of a senator at that."

"Determination can work wonders."

"You ended up finding her in Nevada. Newspaper said you worked fifty-one hours straight to get the job done. And then you just quit? Did she annoy you too?"

"Once I found the girl, I found out that the reason she ran away in the first place was because she was getting molested at home. Happened so often that she finally left a video camera running whenever she was in her room. Caught her illustrious father banging away at her on tape. And when I brought her to the police, the bastard had enough pull with the higher-ups to make the tape disappear and bring her back into the house."

My voice had grown quiet.

"Five hours later, her body was found in the garage. She had turned on the car and lay down to breathe in the exhaust. Seventeen years old. My superior said that's just the way some things work out."

Sergeant Simon's eyes softened for a brief moment.

"That's quite a story, Mister Miller. You're a detective, so I don't have to tell you that Miss Norman's body showed no signs of putting up a struggle. No torn clothing, no skin under the fingernails, no vaginal penetration. That would lend itself to the assumption that she trusted whoever was responsible for this."

"Trust, heavy medication, or stupidity. I'd say those are your three best avenues."

"What was your relationship with Miss Norman like?"

"You mean did she trust me? Probably. She came to me seeking help and she hadn't even known me more than forty-eight hours. Of course, if she came to see me that quickly, I'd start checking into her background, and why she didn't seek the aid of friends or family. If you want alibis, Mr. Jones and I spent the evening eating dinner in the company of two friends."

Everett produced the meticulously folded receipt from the last restaurant we visited and showed it to Lucille.

"Who accompanied you to dinner?" she asked.

"None of your bu-" I started to say but Everett beat me.

"My wife Nicole and his friend Lillian Cassidy," he said. I glared at him but he responded with, "We have no reason to hide anything."

Sergeant Simon continued her question-and-answer session a little while longer and then called in an officer to bring us home, cautioning the two of us to bring forth anything that turned up that might be of substance. After we were dropped off outside the cottage, Everett turned to me.

"They already know where we live. It wouldn't have taken them long to discern who Nicole and Lil are. Being forthcoming with that information should establish a small rapport of trust."

"Wouldn't hurt to make them have to work at finding stuff out. I don't like bringing Lil and Nicole into this."

"Sam, the body was dropped at our cottage. They're already involved." He paused. "Why didn't you tell her you had seen Melissa at the art festival?"

"You were studying that report like it was the original copy of the Bible. What did you notice?"

"Rope burns on the wrists, a deep gash across the throat, woman was fully clothed."

"Any signs of a struggle?"

"Not that I could see from a photograph."

"What was the film quality like?"

"What?"

"The film. Was it of high quality?"

"Yes, Samuel. I was thinking of hiring the police officer to take pictures when Nicole and I renew our vows next September."

"Don't be an asshole. You already acknowledged it was good enough to see the rope burns clearly."

"Fair enough. What's your point?"

"That's not the same woman I saw at the art festival."

"Were you drinking then too?"

"The woman at the art festival had a tattoo of a rose on her ankle. There was no tattoo of that nature on this woman's body.

The dead chick's got a much nicer ass too – but I don't think that would hold up in court."

"So you're saying – "

"There's two Melissa Normans. Or at least two women who look alike. I'm not officially working here, but that might actually be what is considered a clue."

"Wouldn't an item of that nature seriously benefit the sergeant with whom we just spoke?"

"Sure. It'd also give her enough ammunition to seriously tie our hands to her as some sort of material witness. And I'm not spending my vacation at her beck and call."

"I would venture to observe that we have a killer who would present a difference of opinion."

"Yeah, I realize that. Any ideas?"

"You've met three people since you've been here. Two of them are dead. Seems to me we talk with the third one while we still can."

"Abraham Punditt."

"Francis Mortimer Boulet."

"He may just charm the hell out of you."

"I believe that's exactly how his business card reads."

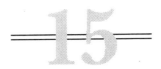

When I woke up the next morning, Lil was painting her toes
out on the deck. Nicole and Everett were still sleeping, so she
had moved the portable radio outside, and as I joined her with
a glass of orange juice, I was met with a hushed blast of Celtic
fiddle music.

"The landlord called while you and Everett were out last
night," she said, switching from her right foot to her left. "He
wanted to know if we planned on having any more corpses on
his front lawn during our stay."

"What'd you say?"

"I told him that this was why we paid cash up front."

"That's my girl."

I recounted our conversation with Sergeant Simon,
whereupon Lil commented that perhaps we ought to invite
Lucille out with us the next time we eat, to ease the tension.

I remarked that with the amount of bodies that were starting to pile up, it might not be advantageous for Lucille Simon to spend social time with us.

"Well then, she's just boring," Lil said, screwing the cap back on her nail polish bottle. "What do you plan to do about this situation?"

"Everett and I thought we'd go talk with Abraham Punditt before he turns up dead on top of my car."

"You have, of course, informed Everett about Abraham Punditt?"

"Yeah."

"And he still thinks it's a good idea?"

"He suggested it."

She put her hand on my shoulder. "My dear, you have hit rock bottom."

"Thank God. It's about time."

She laughed. "Well, at least now you're in familiar territory. Where do you plan on finding Mister Punditt?"

"Everett said he had an office in East Greenwich. Figure we'll start there."

"Will any of this have an adverse effect on my time in the sun?"

"Not at all."

She stretched and stood up. "Well then, good luck."

"No concern for my safety?" I asked as she walked toward the door.

She stopped and turned around. "Babe, you make love with me. If that doesn't kill you, you're set for life."

I smiled and motioned in the direction of the radio, which was still blazing with three or four Irish fiddlers.

"Are we having pangs of longing for our homeland?"

Lil gave me a grin which could blot out the sun.

"Land of me people, boyo. If you have no roots, you have nothing."

And she stepped inside.

East Greenwich, Rhode Island was built on a hill, and people very quickly turned that into such a distinction that living "on the hill" was equated with rising financial status. All I equated it with was a pain in the ass in snowy weather. The town was pretty enough, in an old-fashioned way, but was filled with so many wannabe rich people that if you didn't wear some sort of alligator on your shirt or have "I shop at J. Crew" tattooed across your forehead, people immediately recognized you as an outsider. Kids in East Greenwich did not learn their ABCs, they learned their BMWs, and if you didn't walk with your nose at least halfway in the air, you were told you were slouching. I fit in very well.

At the base of the hill was an old mom-and-pop Main Street filled with, among other things, a theatre, two restaurants, a photographer's studio, five hairdresser salons, a dog groomer, and about seventy-two bridal shops. A lot of people getting married in East Greenwich.

Everett had collected a sheaf of papers with information pertaining to our man Punditt, and he poked through it until he found the address for Abraham's office. I parked the Mustang on the street and Everett and I walked down to Punditt's office.

The office buildings on Main Street were all former family homes that had been renovated to house businesses instead. It was much easier to give over your money in a homey atmosphere. Punditt's office was six blocks down, toward the center of East Greenwich. He had a modest-looking one-story building which was sandwiched between a tax accountant on his left and a Realtor on his right. The placard next to his door read "Abraham Punditt: Spiritual Matters."

I tried the knob. It was locked. I rang the doorbell. Punditt didn't answer. Neither did a secretary. Or a monk dressed in robes. I rapped on the door using the polished gold knocker. I leaned on the bell again. I banged on the door with my fist. Nothing. The shades were drawn on both the front windows, and the stained glass over the door prevented anyone from looking in.

"Got your cell phone?" I asked Everett.

He nodded.

"Call information and get the number for this office."

He did, and as soon as he connected with the building, I heard Punditt's phone ringing inside. After the fourth ring, Everett told me the machine had picked up. He listened to the message and hung up.

"Abraham is closed for the week. His message says he is tending to the affairs of the recently released Albert Crispin and his family, and is then at a conference in Providence for the latter half of the week."

"Recently released?"

"Those were his words."

"He leaves that much information on his answering machine? What happened to confidentiality?"

"Free advertising. He's a businessman, Sam."

"Is there an opportunity to leave a message?"

"Yes."

"Toss me your phone."

Everett handed it over and I hit the redial button. I listened to the same message Everett had just recounted, and when the beep sounded to leave a message, I spoke into the phone.

"Abraham, this is Samuel Miller. I would appreciate you giving me a call. It would probably be in your best interests to do so as soon as possible."

I left my number, hung up, and handed the phone back to Everett.

"Are you trying to scare him?" he asked.

"Yep."

"What now?"

"Let's see how long it takes for our boy to return our call."

We walked back down the street to the Mustang.

As we got into the car, I said to Everett, "Did you see the unmarked car with the whip antenna parked across the street at the donut shop?"

"Yes I did."

"Did you see it pull out and pass by us when we walked away from Punditt's office?"

"Mm-hmm."

"Did you get the plate number?"

"Of course."

"It's probably nothing."

"Probably."

"Could just be a coincidence."

"Lots of those."

"Still wouldn't hurt to check."

"My dear friend," he said as he punched numbers into his cell phone, "I'm already on it."

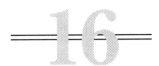

At two thirty-seven, I was sitting on the deck with my feet on the railing when my cell phone rang. The sun was high in the sky and had pleasantly burned my sight into oblivion, and the wind had rocked me onto the verge of a nap. I reached for my cell phone and picked it up.

"Hello?"

"Mister Miller, Abraham Punditt. How good of you to call and check on my welfare during this trying time. The heart of a stranger can be just as warm as the love of a lifelong friend, you know."

"We need to talk, Abraham."

"Certainly, certainly. I agree. I'm holding a remembrance service for Albert this evening at Crispin Fields. I thought it appropriate that it be held there, as it is a physical representation of the love and generosity he felt for this community. Why don't we meet after that?"

"Fine."

"Shall we designate a meeting place and time?"

"I'll go to the service myself, Abraham. I'm sure I'll be able to find you when it's over."

"Very good, very good. I'll see you tonight then, Mister Miller."

"Absolutely."

I hung up.

I sat back in my chair and closed my eyes. I could hear the surf a short distance away. The sun warmed my whole body. The shouts and laughter from the beach rose above the trivial day-to-day sounds of traffic and work, and seemed to batter their way to the top.

Abraham Punditt was somehow connected to, if not involved in, two murders, and tonight I was taking the first step toward becoming a part of whatever it was he had fucked up. I was jealous of the people shouting and laughing below me. They had no cares, no worries for the time being, and they were exactly where I should be. Hell, right now, I was even jealous of Melissa Norman. At least she didn't have to deal with any of this anymore.

An evening listening to Abraham Punditt.

It was going to be a long night.

Crispin Fields was situated in the section of town known as The Pier. It was basically considered the center of town, and the fields were located two streets up from the beach. They were neatly tucked away in back of the elementary school, and to his credit, Albert Crispin had given the town a very nice piece of property. The area was large and quite deep, and the fields were nicely manicured and very well maintained. I parked the car, and before we got out, we could hear Punditt's voice sailing over the commons. We walked to the fields, stood behind the backstop, and watched.

Punditt put on a show. He was dressed in a suit that would make Armani drool, and was hooked up to a sound system that probably garnered him reception in Europe. He had constructed a stage connecting with the dugout, and stood upon it addressing the crowd piled into the bleachers. Three small movie screens were erected around the stage, flashing a progression of slides depicting Crispin at various stages of his life, while Punditt delivered a soliloquy on the wonderful merits of Crispin's time on earth. When I died, I just wanted to be burned to ash and scattered on the ground.

Punditt had a stage presence, I'll give him that. With the lights, and music, and his natural voice, you almost forgot the ceremony was for Crispin. He danced and waltzed back and forth across the stage with an energy that made the Riverdance sound in the back of my head. He had situated the speakers so that his voice actually came down from the heavens, and the audience sat captivated by his antics. I'm sure Oliver Stone was in the audience, taking voluminous notes.

He finished his eulogy to a thunderous barrage of orchestral music, and I was half expecting to see valkyries swoop down and carry the resurrected Albert Crispin off to Valhalla. Instead I was treated to Abraham Punditt donning a robe over his suit that cost more than Israel and then greeting each and every mourner as he or she descended from the bleachers. The cynical side of me was positive I caught him sliding his business card into the pocket of each person he hugged.

Everett and I waited a little over an hour while Punditt dealt with the crowd, and then we strolled across the pitcher's mound to go see a priest. By the time I realized how absurd this really was, I had already made it to second base, which was quite farther than I ever intended to go with any member of the clergy.

When we reached Punditt, he was offering quiet words of consolation to an older woman of obvious stature who had the uncanny ability to turn her grieving on and off so she lamented at only the most appropriate moments. Abraham had guided her through her latest welling-up, and as the spectators had diminished, she deemed it time to put on a strong face and bear her anguish with a strong and noble heart. Abraham shook hands with the final three well-wishers, turned to us with a contented smile, and motioned us up to sit in the bleachers.

"Quite a show," I remarked as we sat down.

"Indeed. The spirit of Albert Crispin was alive and strong in me tonight. He entered my body and used it as a vessel to show his love one last time." He gazed off into the distance. "It truly was an honor to represent him tonight."

Jesus.

I leaned back and put my arms on the bleacher seats behind me. Everett had settled in close to Punditt and leaned forward with his arms resting on his knees, his hands clasped in front of him.

"You're pretty relaxed, Abe, for a guy whose two best friends just got murdered."

He turned and looked at me over his shoulder.

"Don't be crass, Mister Miller," he said. His voice had turned to a high-pitched keen. "Life is a precious gift. It pains me to say good-bye, but one's life should be relished and celebrated as one passes on."

"Life is precious, Francis. Are you running a Britney Spears soundtrack for Melissa's funeral?"

He almost faltered when he stood up but he did manage to look me straight in the eye.

"That's just about enough, Mister Miller," he said. "If you are going to continue to be this caustic, I see no reason to continue this discussion."

And with that, he stormed down the bleacher steps as much as a man wearing Calvin Klein fashion designer low-cut boots can storm.

"Gentleman seems a bit high-strung," Everett murmured.

"Doesn't seem fazed by two murders, though," I replied, standing up and watching him leave the fields. "Maybe it's all that inner peace."

"Two good friends dead and he doesn't ask for help or protection. I was a skeptic, I might wonder why."

"Wonder all you want," I said. I watched as Abraham opened the door to his Mercedes, climbed in, and started it up. "This guy's a fuck. That's the closest biblical quote I can think of to describe him."

We walked down the bleachers and back across the fields to my car.

"Might be a smart move to discuss the character of Abraham Punditt, a.k.a. Francis Boulet with one Lawrence Oakes."

"Why?"

"I would think it might prove beneficial to garner any background knowledge that would help expedite matters concerning this case."

"This case for which we have no retainer, no expense account, and no paying client."

"Sometimes I fear the value of intrinsic actions is lost on you."

Our conversation came to a halt as we came to my car and found two men leaning against the passenger side.

"Can we help you?" I asked.

The streetlights were on, but as all the mourners and Abraham Punditt had left, ours was the only car left in the parking lot. The lot was hidden from the street by a thick grove of trees, and the driveway that led out was on the opposite side.

"Yeah, you can help us," one of the men said as he pushed himself off of my car. He was a large, burly man. He wore a white tank top, blue jeans, and a pair of heavy duty work boots, and had the body of a dump truck. He made a show of walking slowly toward me to emphasize the weight of the boots as well as the girth of his body. The other man was younger, smaller, and thinner, and remained back by the car. He seemed to be watching the other one intently, almost studying him.

Dump Truck came up to where he was looking me straight in the face. "It is time for you to stop dealing with Abraham Punditt. He appreciates your concern but would now like to be left alone."

His voice had a sound like a rototiller stuck in mud. He had trouble with multi-syllabic words like "Abraham" and "appreciate" and you could see him visibly struggling to remember his lines.

"Have some gum," I said, extending a stick.

"What?"

"You smell like Cheetos. If you're going to threaten someone, at least freshen your breath first."

He stared at me.

"Lay offa Punditt. You been warned."

And with that, he slammed his fist into my chest and sent me sprawling back along the pavement. Before I could get up, he came over and kicked me hard in the ribs.

"That's enough," I heard Everett say, and when I looked up in his direction, I could see his gun leveled at my attacker.

"OK," Dump Truck said. "You guys know what's good for you, you'll listen to our warning."

He walked down toward the street and his partner followed him.

"I didn't know you were carrying your gun," I mumbled. My mouth held remnants of gravel from French kissing the asphalt.

"An exercise in caution," he said, watching our attackers blend into the distance. "Somebody leaves a dead body on your porch, I figured it might be a smart move."

Everett came and stood over me. I slowly picked myself up off the ground.

"Sonofabitch broke my sunglasses."

He grinned down at me. "You still want to wait for a retainer?"

The first thing we did the next morning was go buy a new pair of sunglasses. Priorities need to be established at some point. There was a shop across from the beach that sold Ray-Bans, and within twenty minutes, I was a fully equipped detective again. While I adamantly reminded Everett that as we had no expense account, I was already in the hole with this case, he convinced me that there would be a way that my purchase could work its way into being a tax write-off. God bless America.

I was not in a good mood. I was being played for a sucker, and no matter how you rationalized it, that was the final result every time. Lil knew me well enough to leave me alone when I got like this, and she was already at the gym and then she and Nicole were visiting the final day of the Wickford Art Festival. I asked her to keep an eye out for a psycho with blond hair and a rose tattoo on her ankle.

I was wearing my standard work clothes, which consisted of a white T-shirt and blue jeans. The weather was cool today and we had the top down on the Mustang, so I also had a black short-sleeved shirt which I left unbuttoned over the T-shirt. Everett was dressed casually for him, which meant simply that he wore no tie. The creases in his pants were still sharper than my pocketknife.

We cruised in no real hurry up Route 1 into Route 4 and got off at the exit for East Greenwich. Once again we drove down Main Street, but this time, I parked behind a Dunkin' Donuts located past Punditt's office. I explained on the drive up that it was much easier to break into Punditt's office in the afternoon, as no one would think that anyone would be stupid enough to attempt a break-in in broad daylight. Everett responded with some mumbo-jumbo about "standing in plain sight without being seen" and went on to quote Sun-Tzu for the next fifteen minutes, but as long as he wasn't arguing, I couldn't care less. Which is why at eleven thirty in the morning, he and I were walking down Main Street with a foot-long crowbar stashed in his attaché case.

Everett had called from the car, but Punditt's answering machine still picked up. Just to be safe, we knocked on the door and tried to peer in through the windows when we arrived at the office. Satisfied that no one was home, we walked on past it, turned right down the next side street, and then right again to double back on the street below. We came up behind his office, which simply had two windows and a small door. One of the windows had an air conditioner in it, and the door had no outside handle.

Most of the traffic occurred down Main Street, which was in front of the building and us, and the only buildings back on this side looked to be quiet residential homes. I didn't think anyone would call the police on someone as well-dressed as Everett, which is why I didn't object when he volunteered to jimmy the door. He got the crowbar in quietly, wrenched the door open, and gave me a mini-sermon on the value of taking the right vitamins every day, all in under thirty seconds. We walked in quickly and pulled the door behind us.

Everett walked briskly through the entire office, scanning the walls, looking for any sort of keypad. Finding none, he seemed content with the idea that there was no security system, and we allowed ourselves a leisurely look around the office.

We had entered through the back room, which looked to house excess storage as well as a sink, coffeemaker, and small refrigerator. We walked through a small hallway that held a restroom on one side, and what appeared to be an empty conference room and an office on the other. The office had a stained glass window front next to an unlocked door. The inside of the office contained a small desk with a semi-leather/semi-duct taped chair behind it and three burned-out bulbs above it. The front room held the reception area, with a modest desk and phone and two oversized chairs for aspiring clients. There was a stack of magazines between the two chairs that was in a race with the dust in the room to reach the ceiling. The magazines were losing.

"Think Abraham does most of his work from his home office?" Everett said, rifling through some desk drawers.

"Probably donates the housekeeping stipend to some sort of charity," I said.

We took a good look through what little there was before deciding there was nothing of worth in his office. In total mass quantity, I think I had more in the glove compartment of my car. We exited out the back way, closed the door, and walked up the street back to the car.

"It seems we will have to pursue other avenues in order to accumulate any viable data," Everett stated as we crossed the street.

"Look on the bright side," I said. "This is the first place we've been where we didn't find somebody dead."

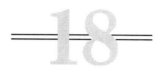

"I got a call this morning on that unmarked car from the other day," Everett said.

We were sitting at an outside bar enjoying two of the largest deli sandwiches I had ever seen. You could hear the sound of the surf from across the street, but the smell of the salt air was blocked by a wall of pungent pastrami and roast beef.

"I'm surprised it took this long. Usually your contacts have information for you before you're finished dialing the phone."

"Sometimes the president is more important than I."

"Hard to believe."

The Thousand Island dressing had seeped into the rye bread, so my sandwich was now completely saturated, making a dripping mess as I bit into it. Perfect.

"Our mysterious car is registered to one Officer Lawrence Oakes."

"No shit," I said, with a mouthful of tomato. "I'm surprised you didn't say 'ta-da' after his name."

"Nothing startling with the fact that it was Oakes, I agree," Everett said as he cut his sandwich into four slices of exactly equal size. "What gives cause for rumination is the fact that the plates on the car are Rhode Island State Police plates."

"So what? So he transferred from Massachusetts to Rhode Island."

"And just happens to be watching Abraham Punditt's office? And watching us watch Punditt's office?"

"I know, I know," I said, mopping up my plate with a crust of rye bread. "There's no such thing as coincidence. All right. Let's go pay a visit to Mister Lawrence Oakes."

Everett looked up at me with a half-smile on his face.

"It would be the logical next step," I said.

"It would." His face beamed a full smile now. "I thought we didn't have a case."

"We don't. We have at least one asshole, though. And he's starting to annoy the hell out of me."

"Took longer than usual."

"Yeah, well, I am on vacation."

"I know. But that's usually when your patience is at its shortest."

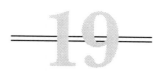

We called the State Police office and were told that Lawrence Oakes was off for today, but had the morning shift tomorrow. He worked out of the State Police Barracks in North Kingstown, which ironically was located right up the road from Wickford. Convenience was nice. Of course, we were in Rhode Island, and inconvenience meant a ride longer than twenty minutes.

Lunch was over, the bill was paid, and half of the day was still unused. I dropped Everett off at the cottage and headed for the gym. I hated to admit it, but Everett was right. I was starting to get aggravated, and with that aggravation came a desire to take care of this situation. For some reason, I was inextricably linked to this case, and until it was resolved, it was going to be hanging over my head, waiting to burst. I'd rather be the one to do the bursting and then get on with my life. However, as we weren't meeting with Oakes until tomorrow morning, I figured I'd take out some of my frustration at the gym. It wasn't as good as hitting Abraham Punditt, but he wasn't available at the moment.

This time of day, the gym was not that busy. The majority of people spent the winter months working out so they could look good during the summer at the beach. That left the gym empty during the summer months when it was prime time for people to be showing off their finely chiseled bodies.

The receptionist greeted me with a smile that said she couldn't remember if I had been here before, but didn't want to offer me a membership in case I had. To that end, she kept the smile and turned up the music as I registered and walked by her. If she had any more things to do, she wouldn't be able to remember what page she was reading in *Cosmopolitan*. God help her if the phone rang at the same time.

I decided to work on triceps today, so I set to work on extensions, pull-downs, and ended with three sets of dips. Then I went over to a corner in the gym and worked on abs. I always worked abs. Hell, with the way I was getting hit in the ribs lately, I might as well.

I finished my workout and walked back across the gym. As I passed the cardio section, I noticed an older man riding the stationary bike, reading the newspaper. The back page of the paper he was reading held a full-page ad that read: **SEEK THE SPIRTUALIZED LIFE. BECOME YOUR IDEALIZED SELF.**

UTILIZE THE GUIDANCE OF ABRAHAM PUNDITT. It went on to list the dates of his convention that was being held at the Westin Hotel in Providence.

The gentleman who was riding the bike noticed me reading his paper and stopped pedaling.

"Are you attending the convention?" he asked. He wiped his forehead with the towel hanging around his neck. He was a large man; not obese, but not layered with muscle either.

"I haven't made up my mind yet," I said. "Do you know Mister Punditt?"

"Mister Punditt," he laughed. "Call him Abraham, my friend! We all do."

Jackpot.

He stepped off the bike and came around and shook my hand.

"Jacob L. Bollock, Esquire. Glad to meet you." He smiled widely.

"Likewise," I said. "How do you know Abraham?"

I didn't want to give him my name, in case he had regular conversations with Punditt. My gut told me that anyone who introduced himself as "Esquire" would talk just to talk if you let him, and wouldn't remember your name even if you provided him with it. My gut proved correct. Probably because I had just spent the last half hour exercising it.

"Abraham helps me lead a more fulfilling life," Bollock responded. "He guides me in day-to-day decisions, monetary transactions, personal matters, everything. My life has become much fuller as a result of that man, I daresay."

I was tempted to look behind me and see if there was a teleprompter feeding him his lines.

"Money, life, and spiritual fulfillment? That's a pretty tall order."

"Ah, a skeptic. Good. The realization of the strength of his program is much more powerful when it is questioned and scrutinized and then finally revealed to be true."

The teleprompter had to be battery operated because I didn't see an extension cord when I walked in.

"I'm a no-nonsense type of man. I hate wasting time," Bollock continued. "I'm the Bollock of Bollock and Fayres, one of the larger law firms in Providence. In short, I don't have time to dally or fool around. But I've spent the better part of the last three years working with Abraham."

"What exactly is his program?" I tried to put on my 'please, tell me more' face. I probably barely managed 'really – I'm a sucker.'

"As I said, he tries to enable you to make decisions that lead to a more enlightening and fulfilling life. I meet with him once, sometimes twice a week. I keep him abreast of all major happenings in my life, and simply ask for guidance and help as life unfolds."

"I'm sure there's a catch. He must charge a pretty penny for his services?"

"Not at all. He's a very generous man. He does charge a flat rate of fifty dollars a meeting, but a man's got to eat somehow, you know? Once he becomes a part of your life routine, he asks that you instead make donations to *Search for Salvation*, his personal fund."

"That leaves it a little open-ended, doesn't it?"

"Absolutely. But once you start living with the results of his direction, you'll want to give him help in assisting others the same way I assure you he'll help you."

We walked over to the front desk, where he retrieved his keys.

"The convention this weekend is an excellent opportunity to check out his program. Why don't you stop by?"

We walked outside to his car, a luxury Cadillac with an all-leather interior. Not a dent or a scratch on it, and freshly washed and waxed. He reached in the open window and returned with a business card, which he handed to me.

"Here's my card. Stop by the convention and give my name at the reception desk. I'll take care of you."

We shook hands and he smiled.

"I hope to see you there," he said, and got in his car and drove off.

Knowing Abraham Punditt was not a good thing. In my personal experience, it had caused a dead body to be left on my doorstep. Knowing Abraham Punditt and supporting his practices was guaranteed not to be a good thing. It could, in fact, be downright criminal.

I stood and watched Jacob L. Bollock, Esquire drive away.

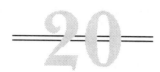

I went back inside the gym, borrowed a towel from the front desk, and took a long shower. Feeling refreshed, impeccably clean, and semi-competent at almost grasping a clue, I got in the Mustang and headed back to the cottage.

Aerosmith's latest album was a collection of old blues covers, and it was one of the best albums I had picked up to date. It was back-to-basics rock 'n' roll. No frills, no accessories, just music. I cranked it up as I left the gym and just let the music from "Honkin' on Bobo" stream out of the speakers and into me.

Lil hated Aerosmith. But that was part of her charm. Perusing the bookshelves at the local Barnes and Noble one time while waiting for a dinner reservation, Lil ended up leaving with a book entitled *Dining with Sharks,* a book on how to profit from a cutthroat attitude. I left with *100 of the Stupidest Things Ever Said.* Later on, Everett would remark that he knew Lil and I would be good for each other because she had said those three simple words. "I love you?" I had asked. "No," he'd replied, "she said, 'His music's shit.'" And people said romance was dead.

I drove around the block before I parked to let the song finish, and then pulled into the driveway up by Lil's Jeep. A breeze had picked up in the afternoon, and as I walked up the steps to the side door, I almost felt a slight chill.

Lil was dressed in cutoffs and a white sweatshirt when I walked in, and had her hair pulled up in a bun with three pencils sticking through it. This usually signified her business mode, a fact made more evident by the three open notebooks arranged on the coffee table and the cell phone in her hand.

She was talking on the cell phone and held up one finger when she saw me walk in. I'm sure she was saying something intelligent into the phone, but I didn't even hear her voice. I was entranced by her walk. Lil moved with a grace and elegance that would put members of the royal family to shame, and watching her walk around the living room as she talked only served to restate the fact that she had a refinement most runway models train their whole life for. At a dinner party a year ago, someone had tried to tell me that I was projecting my own ideals and desires onto Lil and that she really didn't have any of these qualities, as far as he could see. I disagreed, and he spat out two teeth when our discussion was over. Lil recommended that we didn't go back there for dinner in the future.

She finished her conversation, shut the phone off, and turned to greet me. I sat down on the couch and she joined me, sitting on the coffee table.

"I thought you were on vacation," I said.

"I am. This is just minutia from the restaurant. I called Roz to check up on things, and then just took down some information over the phone."

"And how is my number one fan?"

"She says the place is running exceptionally well with you gone. She even suggested that we could turn a considerable profit if you remained out of state for a while."

"Like, for how long?"

"Like, forever," she smiled.

"I always suspected that Roz was secretly carrying a torch for me. She's just playing a little hard to get."

"Oh, most definitely. Here, take a look at these." She handed me the three notebooks. "This is a review of the bands we've had in there the last four months. This one is a record of our food sales by the day for the last week, and this is the liquor inventory for the last two weeks."

"She couldn't just e-mail this to you?"

"She did. I copied it down so you would look at it before the next century."

"I see."

I looked through the finely detailed notes Lil provided me. The review of the bands was obsolete. I knew which ones I liked and which ones I didn't. Nicole and Everett would cross-reference the amount of money brought in by each band with the time of year, and start planning next year's schedule via the information. Lil didn't care; she would simply warn each band that if they played "Mustang Sally" one more time, she would personally start breaking legs.

The food sales spoke for themselves. I didn't even bother looking at them too deeply. Lil and Everett had spent a good part of a year researching various areas and dining out incessantly to find what they considered the best cooks for our venue in the area, and then convinced each one to come work for us. Everett was an expert at managing money, and Lil was an adamant supporter of the theory that you get what you pay for, so the cooks were promptly hired, and profits started to increase.

The liquor inventory was equally immaterial. The only move I had made to increase our liquor revenue was to fire our Tuesday night bartender because he sat around and drank Grey Goose vodka all night long. That move alone saved us hundreds.

As far as I was concerned, if your bar was busy, your help would not have time to drink while working. And keeping your bar busy was a simple combination of good food and service, worthwhile entertainment, and a schedule that catered to being open only during the busy times. Besides, Lil and I screened every applicant personally. It might take a little time, but going that extra mile insured a quality staff that then remained with you for a good amount of time.

"Looks good to me, babe," I said, stacking the notebooks neatly back on the table. "But that's due to your exceptional organizational skills. I'm strictly a worker bee. Put me behind the bar, ask me to find some bands, I'll do that. That's always been my role in this whole endeavor."

"Worker bee, huh?" Lil said, taking the pencils out of the back of her hair and letting the bun unravel, cascading down over her shoulders. "You do know the only function the worker bee has is to service the queen."

She had moved off the coffee table and was now sitting on my lap, facing me with her arms draped lightly around my neck. Her hips started to gyrate ever so slightly.

"It's not a job I take lightly," I said.

"I know," she said as her lips brushed mine. "In fact, I can tell already."

"Ever willing to rise to the occasion of duty."

She leaned in and kissed me.

"Lil, did you show Sam what you picked up at the art festival?"

The door flew open and Nicole bounded into the kitchen. Everett followed her in, carrying a newspaper under one arm and a bag of groceries in the other. Lil stared at the two of them blankly.

"I thought the two of you were spending some time at the library."

You could probably slip in the puddle of disdain that dripped from her voice.

"The town library did not provide ample service for our needs," Everett remarked. "The university library is on summer session, and would've been closing shortly after we arrived there. We'll seize the opportunity to access that venue over the next couple days."

"I'm sure there is a Barnes and Noble somewhere in the area," I said, my voice dryer than the Sahara.

"True, true," Everett said, rummaging through the refrigerator for a drink. "But you can't do everything in one day; otherwise what will you do with the rest of your vacation? Besides, Nicole wanted to show me what she picked up at the art festival."

"Of course. Did you want to show me what you picked up at the art festival?" I asked Lil with resignation.

"I was about to show you something," she said as she dismounted. "Piece of art wasn't exactly what I had in mind."

I had to admit that Lil's taste in things was impeccable, and that was a trait that extended into every avenue of her life. While Nicole cavorted around the living room with her purchases, explaining every artistic nuance to Everett, Lil guided me into her bedroom, where she had stashed her acquisitions. She showed me a watercolor painting of a bouquet of long-stemmed roses that was wonderfully romantic in its simplicity, an aerial photograph overlooking the city of Boston at night, and the black-and-white photograph I had admired earlier of the couple walking the beach in the rain.

"I saw this one," I said, holding it and looking it over.

"Figured you liked it," she smiled.

I had stopped being surprised at moments like this. Lil and I might differ greatly with the superficial things, music, food, etc., but instances like this proved we were right where we should be. Little aspects like what was unspoken in the photo were where we clicked. And what was left unspoken in the photo was basic and primordial. These basics were where we held hands with each other with the strength of a rock. These basics were where we initially and continually clicked. And we both knew it.

"It's Everett's turn to cook," Lil said, taking the pieces back and storing them in the closet.

"Yeah, I saw him carry in a bag of groceries."

"A bag of steamers and six breasts of chicken." She closed the door to the bedroom all the way. "How long do you suppose that will take to cook?"

"Depends on whether Everett tries to light the grill himself or asks Nicole for help."

I was sitting on the edge of the bed. Lil came back and stood in front of me.

"We were about to engage in some frivolous behavior before they arrived." The gleam in her eye would scare the devil.

"Frivolous, but athletic," I said. "Cornerstones of a good healthy life."

"How much did you exert yourself at the gym this afternoon?" she asked, pushing me back on the bed.

"I've got plenty of reserves."

"Good to hear," she said climbing on top of me.

Dinner was late anyway.

21

The State Police Barracks in North Kingstown were housed in an all-brick building that resembled a town hall more than a police barracks. The building was long, red-bricked, and colonial in design. There was a large parking lot in front, and an even larger one in back. The entire area was very well kept, and gave both a stately and welcoming ambiance.

Everett and I arrived bright and early at eight thirty to visit with Lawrence Oakes. We arrived in Everett's vehicle — hoping to make a dignified and regal entrance — parked, and walked in through the front doors. Everett still carried his government-issued ID, and times like this, it worked wonders. Once he presented it at the desk, we were whisked upstairs to see Oakes right away.

The officer on duty led us into a good-sized conference room on the second floor. The room was windowless, but held a long conference table circled by six leather-backed chairs, and state-of-the-art carpeting. Clearly, this wasn't used for interrogating criminals. Or maybe it was. Some of the crooks from Rhode Island I'd read about seemed to be of impeccably high class.

We made ourselves comfortable and within minutes, Lawrence Oakes entered the room. Dropping the government's name could work wonders sometimes. He gave us a broad smile as he walked in. He was a good-sized man, with clear-cut features and a pronounced forehead framed by bright yellow hair shaved military style. He extended his hand to each of us, and took a seat at the far end of the table. He clasped his hands over his stomach, leaned back in the chair, and beamed his grin at us.

"You'll have to excuse me for the smile," he said. "I've been working twelve years on the force, and this is the first time I've ever worked with any G-Men, never mind been personally requested by them."

"We might have kicked the door in a little too hard," I said. "The badge belongs to him," – I motioned to Everett – "he used to work with the Secret Service. I'm a private investigator. We flashed the credentials to hopefully speed up our meeting and not waste anyone's time."

"Sure," he said. "I can respect that. Could I see your license though, please?"

I took out my license and handed it down the table to Oakes. He looked it over and then slid it back.

"What can I do for you guys?"

"We're hoping you can help us with the gentleman Abraham Punditt, a.k.a. Francis Mortimer Boulet."

He snapped to attention like a first-week private. The chair flew forward, and his eyes slammed into ours.

"What has that con artist shit done now? I've had him staked out for the better part of the last six months."

"We know," I said. "You tailed us when we went to knock on his door."

He sat back in his chair and wagged his finger at us.

"Right. I thought you two looked familiar. I didn't place you without your sunglasses. What interest do you have in my man Francis?"

"He seems to be connected with a couple murders."

"Yeah, I knew about Crispin. Who's the other one?"

"Girl named Melissa Norman."

"Never heard of her. How's she connected?"

"Seemed to be an associate of Crispin's and Punditt's."

"Really. 'Curiouser and curiouser' like the girl said. Well, if Francis was anywhere nearby, I guarantee he's dirty somehow. How'd you two come to look into this?"

"Family of Miss Norman asked us to," I lied. "We poked around, and when we checked in on Punditt, your name came up."

"Shit. If Boulet can get nailed, I don't care who does it. What can I do to help?"

"Any information you have on him might lead us somewhere we hadn't thought to look," Everett said.

"Sure," Oakes responded. He was in his territory, and his comfort had become obvious. "What's mine is yours. I'll have Linda run off copies of his file. I've compiled an extensive one on him."

"That was a hell of a lot easier than I thought it'd be," I said, leaning back in my chair.

Oakes winked at me. "We snag him, and I've earned a vacation."

"Funny." I looked at Everett. "We wouldn't even be looking for him if I hadn't taken mine."

Oakes picked up a phone on the wall, pushed a button, and spoke to Linda, asking her to run off copies of Punditt's file. Oakes stayed with us for about five more minutes, detailing the highlights of the file we were about to receive, then excused himself, leaving us to show ourselves out.

We walked downstairs and met Linda at the reception desk, an overweight woman with silver hair who smiled at us generously as she handed us the file. Everett and I turned to leave out the front door. As we walked away from the reception desk, the side door opened, and in walked a somewhat attractive blond wearing a white blouse, green skirt, and sporting what looked to be a rose tattoo on her ankle. If she had a two-inch deep gash across her throat and a puddle of blood beneath her, she would have been a dead ringer for the recently deceased Melissa Norman.

She walked straight in and was about to turn and go up the stairs when she locked eyes with me. A moment of recognition flashed in her eyes, and she turned and bolted back out the door. I moved to chase her, but the hulking figure of Linda had chosen that particular moment to get herself a glass of water from the water cooler, which of course was located next to the stairway by the side door. By the time I maneuvered around her and made it out the door myself, Melissa II was heading for her car, a tiny two-door Spyder. She made it to the car, turned it over, and sped out of the parking lot, leaving me wondering why I even bothered to go running every morning.

Everett joined me in the parking lot as I watched her car speed northward on Route 1A.

"Was that the Melissa Norman look-alike?"

"Mm-hmm."

"The girl who looks just like the dead girl who was left at your door?"

"Yep."

"The dead girl who is somehow connected to one Abraham Punditt who we came here to speak to Lawrence Oakes about?"

"Absolutely." I was still staring down the street.

"And this girl who looks like the dead girl just showed up at the same building where we came to speak to the one man who is an expert on the guy who is suspected of being involved in the murder of the dead girl."

"Give me a minute to write all that down, but I think so, yeah."

"Damn. I'd say that almost looks like a clue."

I looked at Everett. I had a splitting headache.

"This vacation absolutely fucking blows."

22

Upon returning to the cottage, we were reminded by the ladies that while saving the world from overzealous evangelists was indeed admirable work, it wasn't so important that it should detract from making sure that they were enabled to properly enjoy their vacation. That being said, we headed out that evening to a small BYOB restaurant two blocks up the street from the beach. We parked along the Sea Wall, and walked the short distance to the bistro, where we enjoyed a meal of Alaskan king crab and the most expensive soup of which I had ever partaken. It was a slow night, and the restaurant was quiet. When we left, there was only an elderly pair talking over a half-filled bottle of wine, and two college kids in the back finishing up a couple of hamburgers.

Out on the street, the night air was cool, and with a quarter of the moon high in the sky, we decided to walk down toward

119 - 119 -

the beach. There were a handful of cars parked on the side of the street and a few tourists came down the stairs from the Coast Guard House restaurant as we walked by. We passed under the empty Towers, down the curving sidewalk, and crossed into the giant parking lot for the Narragansett town beach. The gate was left unchained, and we walked down the wooden steps onto the beach.

"A little romance is nice, Sam," Lil said as she steadied herself with my shoulder and removed her shoes.

We walked down the beach away from traffic, guided by what little light there was in the sky. The surf resounded quietly around us, and it would've been nice to simply let the moment speak for itself, but of course Everett had to elucidate on the nature and background of each of the few constellations visible in the sky. Nevertheless, it made for a nice night and a little peace and quiet was due right about now.

We walked past some small dunes tufted with grass, and the miniature boardwalk with the closed-up snack shop. A little ways further, the beach curved around and a series of dunes rose up to our left. Off to our right, we could see the lights on the Newport Bridge, where Nicole said we needed to visit sometime in the next week. We walked a little further and then decided to turn around and head back, matching pace with the lights of a ship off in the distance.

The four of us were about a hundred feet from the gated entrance when we saw two people moving down the beach in our direction. We were already on the hard sand by the water, and as they moved down toward us, I recognized them as the two college kids who were in the restaurant earlier. Both of them wore large oversized T-shirts and blue jeans, and their arms hung by their sides as they walked. One had a short buzz cut, and the other wore his hair longish, down to his shoulders. They stopped in front of us.

"We need to talk," Buzz Cut said.

Lil hadn't said anything about dining etiquette when she saw I was taking her out to dinner with my shirt untucked. Everett had been right earlier – it was stupid to go out unarmed with all that had happened so far. Everett and Nicole were standing in front of me, blocking me from the view of our would-be conversationalists, and I reached around underneath my shirt and pulled out the gun I had strapped to the back of my belt. No such thing as being too careful. Of course my shirt was extremely fashionable and even untucked made me look dashingly handsome.

"Put the gun down, Mister Miller."

The voice came from behind me. I turned and looked into the face of the "student" who had watched Dump Truck kick the shit out of me after Everett and I attended Abraham's moving eulogy to Albert Crispin. Apparently, he had come off the dunes and up behind us in the sand while we were distracted by the two up front. Normally, I would have simply asked him to shoot me for my sheer stupidity at being caught off guard, but instead of me, his gun was pointed straight at Lil's head. His eyes never left my direction, but he slowly walked over to Lil, and with the gun now touching the back of her head, stood to the side of her, holding her arm above the elbow.

"Now that we have your attention," he said, "as the boy said, we need to talk."

His grip on Lil's arm was simply for stage presence. It wasn't that tight, because he thought she would be frozen with fear. Shithead. Lil swung her arm back and grabbed his groin as hard as she could. Lil had a manicure once a week. I knew how strong her nails were. I almost flinched with him.

Out of reflex, his body hunched over, and Lil moved away. I turned toward him and fired three shots into his chest. He fell to the ground. Lil didn't make a sound. The shots were enough of a distraction to allow Everett to grab the second one. The third one ran.

He was fast.

I was better.

I chased him down the beach and put two shots into his leg. He hit the ground with a moan. I grabbed a fistful of hair and dragged him into the water. I was in up to my knees. He couldn't even stand. I pushed his head underwater and held it there. I pulled him back up coughing and sputtering.

"What's your name?"

A wave crashed over him. I held his head under again. I pulled him back up and he was gasping for breath.

"What's your name?"

"Le-Leroy," he wheezed.

"C'mere, Leroy."

I dragged him back up the sand to where Everett and the girls were. Lil had taken a gun off the dead one and held it freely by her side. Everett held the second one in a half nelson grip. I dropped Leroy in the sand and looked at the one Everett was holding. He held my gaze. I kicked him in the groin and he went down like a stone. Everett picked him up. I kicked him again. He went down again. Everett picked him up again.

"License says his name is Maurice Sanders," Nicole said, holding up his wallet.

"License? You carry your license with you? Listen to me, Maurice Sanders," I said, tilting his chin up so he looked at me. "Don't you ever, *ever* threaten people I care about. Do you understand me?"

Maurice gave a slight nod.

To the side of me, Leroy groaned.

"He's bleeding bad, Sam," Everett said, looking at Leroy.

"If you're worried about him, call 911. What's the reason for this Maurice? Who sent you?"

Maurice shook his head.

"Look around you, Maurice. Look at your friends. Look at my eyes. I will kick you. I can shoot you. I will beat you. I will win. Who sent you?"

Silence.

I shot Maurice in the foot. Maurice howled in pain. Everett held him upright. I pointed my gun at Maurice's forehead.

"Last chance. My patience is done. Who. Sent. You."

"Lawrence," he stammered. "Lawrence Oakes."

I looked at Everett.

"A former friend of Francis."

"Say that five times fast."

Everett let Maurice go. He dropped to the ground, ripped off his shirt, and wrapped it around his foot. Nicole had his gun as well as his wallet, so we walked back up the dunes to the gate, up the stairs, and into the parking lot. When we were around the corner and heading back toward the car, I gave Everett my cell phone.

"Call 911."

He did.

"A tad excessive, Sam."

"Don't threaten my family."

"The way they ran, they were just kids, not professionals."

"Good. We scare them enough now, they never become professionals."

Nicole looked over at me. "That rationale almost makes your actions sound noble, Sam." She smiled.

"Give me a medal."

Lil took my hand. Her body smelled of the salt water she had used to wash off any residual blood. The guns were in her purse, which hung over her shoulder. She carried her shoes in her left hand. She leaned in and rested her head on my shoulder as we walked.

We heard the ambulance siren in the distance.

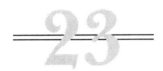

We took turns in the shower when we got back to the cottage. We gave the girls the first round while Everett and I sat out on the deck.

"Nicole all right?" I asked.

"She's a forensic psychiatrist, Sam."

"I know. Lil asked her to analyze me once."

"What'd she say?"

"That if she found out what made me tick, neither you, her, nor Lil would like me anymore, and you three were the only friends I had."

Everett grinned. "My girl took pity on you."

"Doesn't happen often."

"Nope. Just 'cause she's a shrink doesn't mean she sits behind a desk all day. She's a *cop* shrink. And more often than not, she's requested by the cops to join them in the high-pressure situations. Her analysis of the situation and/or the person might lead to a more productive resolution than say, shooting someone in the leg or the foot."

"Don't start."

"Tense situations don't scare her. She thrives on them. Guaranteed there was a part of her analyzing those three punks tonight. We go to bed, she's gonna spend a good hour and a half discussing what type of background and upbringing would lead those kids to be in those particular circumstances and what character traits they are seeking to add to their own collective unconscious."

"You two and your sexy pillow talk."

Lil came out into the living room wearing a fluffy white robe and drying her hair with a towel. Nicole followed about five minutes later wearing a sweatshirt and pajama bottoms.

"Your turn, boys," she said as she went into the kitchen.

Everett took his shower in a water temperature that would make Africa seem frigid, so by the time I finally got to use the shower, any water that was left over took shape in the form of icicles that bounced off my chest. Two Eskimos handed me my towel when I was finished. I came back out to the living room, where everyone was seated and enjoying a plate of fruit, cheese, and crackers Nicole had prepared. We found a TV station that was running an Animal Planet marathon on predators of the jungle and put that on for background noise as we attempted to return to a sense of normalcy.

Our adrenaline buzz wore off, our tensions eventually subsided, and after an hour and a half of mindless chatter from the television, we cleaned up the living room, put the dishes in the sink, locked the doors, and moved off to our respective rooms for the night. Everett and I had agreed to both keep a gun by the bed just in case, but given the emotional and physical states of our would-be attackers, we figured we'd be all right until morning, at which point we'd bring the fight to Lawrence.

Lil and I went into our bedroom. I shut the door and Lil dropped her robe. She was very comfortable with her nakedness, and from my vantage point she had every right to be. She picked up a few stray articles of clothing around the room and hung them up. Then she pulled the covers down and climbed into bed. I stripped off my clothes, turned off the light, and joined her.

As I settled in under the sheets, Lil moved over and put her head on my chest.

"Were you scared tonight?" she asked.

"Sure," I said. I ran my fingers up and down her back. "If I wasn't scared, that'd mean I didn't care, I had nothing to lose."

She played with my chest hair.

"You called me 'family'."

"Oh Christ, babe, relax. I wasn't proposing or anything."

"I didn't say I didn't like it."

We lay there in the dark listening to each other's breathing, feeling each other's heart beat.

"You conflict me. I grew up learning you can't trust anybody. I've relied on myself my whole life." Her words weren't rushed. They came out in a measured rhythmic pace. She'd been thinking about this for a while.

"I wasn't scared tonight. I've been in worse situations. But I liked the fact that you were there to take care of me."

"'Course I was there to take care of you. I don't care about much. You actually matter."

"That's not true. I've watched you work. I've seen you interact with others. You may try to hide it, but you do care about people."

"Different circumstances. I don't like seeing people taken advantage of. Doesn't mean I'd fire three bullets into someone's chest because they caused a skinny blond to cry."

"Mmmmm. Sometimes I think you would. Or at least there's a part of you that would want to."

We lay there in silence. No cars passed outside. No waves crashed. Even the crickets were absent.

She shifted to look up at me, even though I couldn't see her in the dark.

"Does it ever bother you that I was a hooker?"

"No."

"We've been together for a little over two years and you've never mentioned it. Sometimes I wonder what goes on in your head."

"Whatever you were in the past made you what you are now. I like what you are now."

"It shouldn't be that simple."

"Sorry. It is."

"I know."

She put her head back down on my chest.

"I love you, Samuel."

"I know. I love you too."

"Sometimes it scares me. I'm afraid I don't love you back enough. Or the right way. Or that I might not be able to."

"This is a first. I've never seen you insecure, babe."

I stroked her back.

"I was alone a long time before I found you," I said.

"You were an orphan."

"Still am."

I kissed the top of her head.

"Lil, you know as well as I do that in some ways, we will always be alone. We were born alone and we'll die alone."

She moved her fingers over the scars on my stomach.

"But I don't plan on leaving."

"You won't, will you," she said. It was a statement, not a question.

"No."

She stopped moving. Her head rested on my chest.

"You're a good man, Samuel."

"I am for you. If I didn't like you, I'd probably be a big pain in the ass."

"You are a pain in the ass." She leaned in and kissed my neck. Then she kissed my lips. She moved on top of me and kissed my chest and then began moving lower.

"You keep that up and I might get a little excited."

She stopped momentarily and glanced up at me.

"Well it's about time."

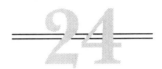

I sat out on the deck looking out at the water. It was a little after six A.M. The surf was calm. The wind was still. Up and down the street, cars were parked silently in their driveways. I breathed in some of the salt air mixed in with a lack of exhaust and let it out slowly.

Lil had calmed me down during the night. She was good at that. She could create peace. Offer contentment where others couldn't. But I didn't want contentment right now. I wanted anger. It was time to go looking for a fight. Contentment and complacency were long gone. It was time to start disrupting things.

I sat back and closed my eyes. I thought about Lawrence Oakes. He'd duped me. I'd been played for a sucker. I pictured him smiling after we left his office. I pictured him calling his cronies to harass us. They had tried to hurt Lil. He had tried to hurt Lil.

I pictured Abraham Punditt. That miserable fuck of a puppet had used me. I had been suckered by Howdy Doody with a halo. I pictured the guns pointed at us on the beach. I pictured the gun pointed at Lil's head. She had trusted me. I pictured her splattered with the gunman's blood. He had tried to hurt Lil.

I opened my eyes.

It was time to go to work.

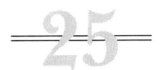

I was showered, dressed, and freshly alert as I turned the Mustang onto Ocean Road and cruised along the water. There was no harm in taking the scenic route to the State Police Barracks; Oakes wouldn't be in until eight o'clock or shortly thereafter, so I had a little time to kill. Even an early bird still has to wait for the worms to wake up.

I pulled into the parking lot a little after eight and found it moderately filled with cars. This was no surprise; police barracks never closed down. I parked in front, the attendant buzzed me in, and I walked right up the stairs. I entered every office on the second floor, but there was no Lawrence Oakes. There was a young officer with more gel in his hair than I thought a crew cut needed, and a larger, older, rounder officer finishing up a bagel and getting most of the cream cheese in his mustache, but no Lawrence Oakes. There was a desk situated next to a wall with hanging citations bearing Oakes's name on them, but there was no Lawrence Oakes at the desk. The desk itself was devoid of any clutter that could be useful in determining his whereabouts. Not even a coffee stain.

I walked back down the stairs to the main entrance hall. Big Linda was already at her post behind the reception desk checking her e-mail and organizing her paper clips.

"Lawrence Oakes, please," I said.

Linda jerked her head up.

"Oh my goodness, you startled me."

"Lawrence Oakes."

"Yes, I believe ...I don't think he's in today."

"Where is he?"

"Well I don't know. He called in earlier stating that he was taking a personal day. But I'm really not allowed to – "

Linda had an inbox, an outbox, stacks of files, mail, and stacks of paper on her desk in front of her. I pushed all of that over the side and watched it clatter to the floor. The only two objects remaining on her desk were her computer and her telephone.

"There," I said, "your day's been cleared. I want Lawrence Oakes. Give me an address, a phone number, call him up and put him on speakerphone, I don't care. But I want him now."

I felt the officer come up behind me and turned to face him. It was the older cop with the mustache I had seen upstairs.

"Time to go, buddy," he said quietly, nudging me toward the door with his shoulder. I let him nudge me. Getting in a fight with the police at police headquarters would do nothing to improve my circumstances. He was being much more patient than I deserved in the first place.

He walked me out the door, and we stood in the parking lot.

"Getting detained for pushing around a secretary is an extremely stupid reason to go to jail," he said. "Don't make me arrest you."

He went back inside.

"I didn't let your partner shoot me."

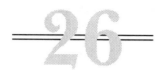

I was ready to start running in circles. I had worked myself up and was now bursting at the seams to the nth degree. Patience was not my strong suit. I had been pushed around enough, and now I was ready to start pushing back. Problem was, unless I found a vehicle through which I could focus my energy, I was likely to start pushing blindly, and the probability that that would lead to reckless behavior where someone got hurt was huge.

I walked up the stairs of the back deck and entered the cottage through the sliding glass door to the living room. Lil was in the kitchen washing some dishes.

"Where have you been?" Lil asked without turning around.

"I went to pay a visit to Mister Lawrence Oakes."

Lil did not acknowledge my presence by looking in my direction. Instead, she whirled around and threw a dinner plate straight at me. It smashed against the wall next to me, about three inches from my head.

"Do not – do *not* go off to do something dangerous and not tell me."

"You were asleep!"

CRASH! Another plate shattered just over my shoulder.

"I figured that was where you went. Do you think I'd try to stop you? I couldn't stop you if I wanted to! But I have a right to know when you are intentionally putting yourself in harm's way!"

"You mean like right now?"

CRASH! A teacup exploded on the wall, covering me in china shrapnel.

"NO SECRETS! We made that promise, Samuel. You are obsessive, you are stubborn, and you are going to do what you want. But I have a right to know when you are placing yourself in jeopardy!"

CRASH!

"Babe –"

CRASH!

"Do *not* make me worry about what *might* be happening to you again!"

Her green eyes were glowing. Steam rose from her body. If I breathed the wrong way, she would kill me on the spot.

"I didn't mean to make you worry," I said. "This thing has exploded in my face, and it's time to put a stop to it. Now."

"I know that. But do not try to go behind my back again."

"I won't. We wouldn't have anything left to eat off of if I did."

The University of Rhode Island's main campus is located in Kingston, which is ten minutes outside of Narragansett. In fact, the cottage we had rented for the month was rented out to URI students during the academic year. Of course, what we were paying per week was what students probably paid for three months during the off season. Things like that helped explain the perspective on real estate in Rhode Island. It also helped to explain the beer stains on the ceiling in our living room.

What was once touted as the "Number One Party School in America" was actually quite picturesque during the summer session. Devoid of students, one could enjoy the lush greenery and stoic architecture of the campus. As Everett and I took a drive around the perimeter, we were greeted by everything from buildings seemingly constructed during medieval times to ultramodern structures that encapsulated their classrooms in wraparound glass.

While the college grounds were indeed very nice to look at, they were not at all driver friendly. After driving in circles for about twenty minutes, we encountered two women who were able to give us the most direct route to access the library. We pulled into a giant parking lot off of Flagg Road, and crossed the access road to the side stairs to URI's library.

The building itself was an impressive-looking edifice, and its entrance faced the heart of the university, as if it was watching over all the academic buildings that were its brothers and sisters. Everett and I mounted the steps and entered through the large glass-paned doors.

"What exactly are we looking for?" he asked.

"I'm hoping you know it when we find it."

"Aren't you supposed to be the detective?"

"I am the detective. All that means is I don't mind being shot at. It has nothing to do with intelligence. For that, I bring along you."

"I see."

Stepping into the foyer, you were struck by how immense a building the URI library actually was. Simply put, you had four stories of intelligence at your beck and call. To your left was the reception desk with three clerks working. To your right was a giant glass wall enclosing a strictly enforced "quiet room" utilized for studying. Directly in front of us were over a dozen computer terminals garnering each individual user access to the stores of knowledge housed in the building. Beyond them was the Current Periodical section, and to the right of that were staircases leading both up and down into the tombs of information amassed inside the complex.

"We've got Abraham Punditt, a.k.a. Francis Mortimer Boulet. We have Lawrence Oakes and we have Melissa Norman's sister. And I just met a Jacob L. Bullock, Esquire. We find a way to connect two or more of them, and that might lead us in the right direction."

"You are explicitly generous with that word 'we.'"

"You signed on to this case long before I did."

"True."

"And besides, you're the only one of the two of us who can work a computer."

We sat down at one of the cubbies and Everett fired up the computer. The computers at the library were hooked up to the database of the library itself. After entering your search, any material that was housed in that building would be listed on the screen with the call numbers, leading you to the copy of each particular document.

Everett began tapping on the keys, making notes on some paper as he went. I looked around at the few people who were in the library. During the summer session, nobody seemed to be that worried or stressed over courses and papers. A group of twelve people came through the library on a guided tour of the campus. The tour guide spoke in hushed tones, in case any of the six people in the building would be disturbed by her five-minute speech of what her group would see here if they had actually visited the school during an academic session.

Everett got up from his chair and motioned for me to follow. We walked past the staircases and straight into the Periodicals section.

"I cross-referenced all the names you gave me in our search, hoping something would arise that would connect at least two of them."

"Any success?"

"I think so."

He led me through the winding shelves that stored all the magazines the library had collected over the years. The periodicals were collected in upright cardboard stands and arranged under a numerical system that made learning Ancient Greek look appealing.

"What exactly are we looking for?"

"Right.......here," he said, scanning the shelf. He referred to his notepad, searched the collections, looked back on his notes, leafed through one set of magazines, and pulled out an issue.

"*The Ocean State?*"

"Yes. It's a magazine which covers goings-on in Rhode Island. And if I understand this to be what it is, this will be very enlightening."

"Goings-on?"

"Shut up, Sam."

We walked to a table in back of the aisles of journals, and Everett flipped through until he found what he wanted.

"There we are," he said, placing the open pages down in front of me.

Three different articles were featured on these two pages. The one on the far right was the one Everett pointed out to me. The picture featured Melissa Norman, who was standing behind her sister. Her sister was dressed in a white, flowing bridal gown, and holding hands with Lawrence Oakes, who was smartly dressed in a black tuxedo. I didn't recognize the fourth face, but the four of them were standing on an outcropping of rock with the beach behind them. The caption below the picture read: "*Classic* magazine mogul Lindsey Norman weds Lawrence Oakes in September." I flipped to the cover. The issue was from 2001.

The article was brief. It stated when the wedding took place and where. Twin sister Melissa was Lindsey's maid of honor, and Greg Landers was the best man.

"What's *Classic* magazine?"

"I'm not sure."

I looked back at the picture.

"Married."

"Yes."

Lindsey's gown flowed to the ground in a very stylish fashion. It still didn't do much to hide her fat ass. Her smile looked like it was plastered on her face. Oakes stood woodenly next to her, squinting into the camera. Melissa stood behind her sister, bright-eyed and full of life, looking twice as elegant as the bride. Her smile electrified the photo. I looked back at the face of Lindsey Oakes.

"I like this woman less and less."

I had never read *The Ocean State* before, but apparently you had to be something important in what Everett had termed "the goings-on in Rhode Island" to be featured in it. In her heyday, *Classic* magazine mogul Lindsey Norman-Oakes was such a person.

The basement floor of URI's library housed a computer network with all the trimmings. As this was the summer session, we had no problem gaining access to a computer and searching the Internet for information on *Classic* magazine.

Everett worked his magic again, this time with much quicker results.

"It would seem Mrs. Oakes's magazine started out with tremendous success," recited Everett as he scanned an article, "and then died out into quiet obscurity."

"Kind of like my sex life since your intrusion into my vacation."

"Don't be ridiculous," he said without even looking at me. "The walls in our cottage are embarrassingly thin."

Everett found what we needed, printed out the articles, and paid the clerk at the desk. I followed him out the door, and we made our way up the hill to the quad at the center of campus. We found a bench next to an old, rustic cannon, and sat. Everett took time to admire the architecture of his surroundings while I read the printouts.

Classic magazine lasted two and a half years. It was a magazine dedicated to spotlighting the "hometown famous" in the Northeast area. Lindsey Oakes, then Norman, had started the magazine in 1999. She started running articles about local celebrities — the mayor, local rock bands, cable access shows, and such. As her readership grew, so did her celebrity status, to the point where she was publishing issues intermixing interviews with the President of Johnson and Wales with members of the Boston Red Sox and Stephen King.

In mid-2002 she ran an expose detailing an elaborate money laundering scandal in Rhode Island, naming four prominent attorneys as the key players in the event. Apparently, she published her story before accumulating all the hard evidence, and the lawyers were able to sue her for libel. The fact that it was a pack of four lawyers whose egos had been bruised and tortured by her reports made certain that the lawsuit bled the magazine dry, forcing *Classic* magazine to die in bankruptcy.

I folded the papers in half and handed them back to Everett.

"What do you think?" he asked.

"We tied Oakes and Punditt together, now we can extend that chain to include Lawrence and Lindsey."

"Mm-hmm."

"Kind of like fitting together three puzzle pieces in a 2,000-piece puzzle."

"It's a start."

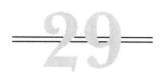

As much as I hated to admit it, Everett was right. We did have a start, albeit a very small one. The next step was tying them together and seeing how they fit in the larger picture. Fortunately, we had a catalyst to enable us to trudge down that direction, in the form of one Jacob L. Bollock.

I dug his business card out of my gym bag. It had three phone numbers on it. Obviously, he was an important man. If I had a lesser constitution, I probably would have been wobbly in the knees just looking at it. I dialed the first number, and on the second ring, a woman picked up and stated, "Bollock and Fayres" in a crisp, professional manner.

"Mister Jacob Bollock, please," I answered.

"I'm sorry, he's busy. May I take a message?" Her reply was automatic. Something told me she only had a couple responses from which she could choose all day long.

"I'm crushed. Jake told me I could call him at any time and he'd take care of me."

"Mister Bollock is a very busy man," she said in a very serious tone. "Perhaps I could help you?"

She did not sound too enthused about the prospect.

"We spoke earlier at the gym. I expressed interest in Abraham Punditt's conference this weekend and he said he could probably get us in."

"That shouldn't be a problem. How many did you need?"

If her elocution was any more wooden, I would have thought I was speaking to an oak tree. I was certain she had a flow chart in front of her directing her to the proper rejoinder for each aspect of a conversation.

"Four would be wonderful."

"And your name, sir?"

"Exuberance."

"Very well, Mister Exuberance. You will have four tickets to the conference, courtesy of Mister Bollock, waiting for you at the front desk of the Westin Hotel in Providence, and I will call ahead and reserve you and your party two rooms. Is there anything else I can do for you?"

"Are you free Saturday night?"

"I'm sorry, sir; our office closes at five o'clock on Saturday."

"I see."

Nothing got past her.

I thanked Bollock's secretary for her time, hung up the phone, and sat back in my chair. Hearing nothing but silence, I became keenly aware of the fact that there was no one in the cottage to congratulate me on the great strides I was making as a master detective. With that in mind, I left a note for Lil, telling her to pack her bags for a weekend of shopping in Providence, and took myself out for a drink.

Providence, Rhode Island is not a huge city, but what it packs into such a small area is impressive. One would not think that a city of its size could carry such an array of schools, businesses, world headquarters, cultural ambience, fine dining, theatres, art, and crime. My money said Abraham Punditt would provide us with at least a few of these items before our weekend was over. Of course, with what I was getting paid for this case, I couldn't afford to cover much.

The sun was setting softly in the sky as Lil and I cruised up Interstate 95.

"So, if Oakes and Punditt are in fact working together, what will this sojourn accomplish?"

Lil wore a yellow and red sundress and was the picture of contentment as she leaned back in her seat and crossed her legs.

"Oakes and Punditt are definitely in something together. And apparently we're perceived as enough of a threat to warrant hiring some wannabe thugs to shut us down."

"Only you don't know why you're being perceived as a threat, because in actuality, you have no idea what they are into in the first place."

"When you say that, you make us sound fundamentally clueless, you know that?"

"Not a good trait in a detective."

"Not at all. What I'm hoping is if we poke around enough in Providence, we'll stir up something that will lead us to something else."

"Kick up enough dirt in the playground and see who comes to tell you to knock it off?"

"That's the plan."

"That's the best plan you've had," Lil said, looking out the window.

"I know."

"That's sad."

We passed a billboard reminding us to watch the evening news. Five smiling faces beamed down at us advising us to tune in at 5:30 and 11 P.M.

"You did say cluelessness was an undesirable trait in a detective," Lil sighed into the window. "What type of trait would be beneficial?"

"Annoying."

"Well," Lil patted my thigh. "There you're at the top of your class."

We swerved up around a curve on the highway and saw the city sprawled out before us up ahead. After darting through a suicidal weave zone, we garnered access to the off ramp, and entered the Renaissance City. Providence was a maze of one-way streets, which was probably intentional, forcing commuting tourists to see all of the sights whether they wanted to or not. Luckily for us, the Westin Hotel was right off the ramp, and within ten minutes, we were parking on the fourth floor of the adjoining garage. I picked up the two bags Lil had in the back seat. Lil popped the trunk, pulled out one more of her suitcases, and handed me mine, which was basically a gym bag I flung over my shoulder.

"You do realize we're only here for the weekend," I said as I shut the trunk.

"That's why I only packed three bags."

We walked down one level and entered the Westin through the parking garage access door. Once we shut the door behind us, we shut reality behind as well. The cold and indifferent gray steel was replaced by a warm and inviting embrace. Plush carpets lined the floors, chandeliers and crystals shined from the ceilings, hotel staff moved about in a relaxed but professional atmosphere, smiling at you as if just being there was making your stay more pleasant already. Lil and I walked down the hall toward the escalators. The railings gleamed in spotless gold, and the stairs moved noiselessly to bring us down to the main foyer.

We descended the escalator and arrived in the foyer, a large rotunda encapsulated in glass and quiet music. To our left was the reception desk, decorated in marble, and staffed with four clerks directing each individual to his or her room with a beaming countenance. To our right was a revolving door that led outside. Standing at attention at either side of the doorway were bellhops looking like they were taken right out of the Sunday afternoon movie: red jacket, brass buttons, even a little hat. Directly in front of us was a parlorlike setting, complete with leather sofas and armchairs, coffee tables, newspapers, and, to make it complete, Nicole and Everett.

"You forget your smoking jacket?" I asked as we walked over to them.

"Splendid accoutrements here, Samuel," he said, folding his paper neatly and placing it back on the table. "One receives superb treatment within the hotel, and has access to the various offerings of the city itself. There's a great deal of history in Providence."

"Might be an exam when we check out. Any trouble getting the room keys?" I asked.

"None at all, sugar." Nicole rummaged through her purse and produced two plastic cards which she handed to me. "We're on the tenth floor. Rooms 1018 and 1020."

"Tenth floor? Bollock's not as big as he thinks he is."

"Be happy with that, Sam," Everett responded. "The hotel's almost sold out. All the conference rooms are at maximum capacity in terms of attendance. Whatever this gentleman does, it seems to be impressive."

"We've been sitting here for the last hour watching people come in. Everyone's well-dressed. Everyone's immediately recognized when they arrive. Everyone walks like they own the place. A lot of power is collected in this building tonight, Samuel."

I looked at Nicole. "I'm so glad Everett married a shrink."

"Observant *and* bright," she smiled. "Not just merely stunning."

"You spot Oakes or Punditt?" I asked Everett.

"No. But we're at the tail end of the arrival time. Everyone's at the Welcome Reception for the time being. That lasts until nine. It's basically a meet and greet, an overview of the conference, and a recognition of various accomplishments and odds and ends."

"Where's this all taking place?"

"Second floor. The main conference room is there."

"Where's the closest bar?"

Everett smiled. "Right across the hall."

"Really. Nicole, we have a hotel full of self-important individuals whose egos are all probably the size of small cities. In your professional opinion, what are the chances that these people might stop off for a beverage before getting ready for a rousing weekend of prayer with Abraham Punditt?"

"You really have to ask?"

"Might give us an opportunity to see what we're up against," I said to Everett.

"Shit," Lil said. "I could've told you that."

Our room was not as extravagant as the lobby would lead you to believe. If Lil had actually filled all three suitcases, there might not have been enough closet space. Luckily, she planned on filling half a suitcase with newly acquired purchases while she was in the city, and thus had room to hang her garments.

The rest of the room was standard. Queen size bed, bureau and mirror, two armchairs, and a small desk complete with complimentary hotel stationary. Lil would say it was passé, while I would maintain it was three times what I deserved. Hence, it was standard.

I looked out the window and down at the view of the curb. Providence had a way of erecting buildings close enough so your view was never allowed to stray too far from where you already were. Probably its own form of crowd control. I drew the blinds while Lil unpacked, and started sifting through the welcome folder that had been left on our bed.

Punditt's *Search for Salvation* was described at as non-profit ministry dedicated to helping people utilize their full spiritual potential. One paragraph delved into Punditt's accomplishments, centering on television appearances and a few gala events, and the rest was filled with quotations from members of his church, stating how wonderful Punditt's ministry was, and how it had revolutionized their lives in ways they had never dreamed. There were pictures of some prominent people from New England next to their statements, but other than that, the welcome packet was basically a tutorial of how *Search for Salvation* could help the new recruits.

"Babe, have you ever felt as if you were 'standing on the precipice of hell and damnation with a weight of sinful priorities bundled to your back?'"

"Every day, dear," Lil replied as she hung up her clothes.

"Well then, it might be advantageous for you to go sit in on some of Punditt's lectures."

She turned around. "I was wondering when you were going to get to my role in this whole endeavor."

"Oakes and Punditt already know Everett and me. They're not going to recognize you or Nicole. If you two go in and watch his performance, you may see something or someone that can help us figure out what's going on."

"You sure? I mean, you are the accomplished detective. I'm just a former hooker."

"Yeah, but you're the one with the brains."

"And yet I remain with you," she smiled.

"God knows why."

"Maybe I'll ask Him during one of these sessions."

"I don't think that's an answer even religion can provide."

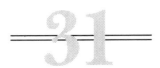

The bar on the second floor of the Westin was large. Considering that it catered to conferences in the hotel as well as the general public, it needed to be. Nicole, Everett, Lil, and I arrived a little after eight. The dinner crowd was thinning out, and the after-dinner crowd had not yet arrived, and as such we had no problem getting a table. We seated ourselves in the far back corner of the ballroom, at a table that was partially hidden by an array of tall potted plants situated to give the illusion of separation between the tables and the makeshift stage against the wall. The lights were dimmed very low, and we had a decent view of the main bar, which was diagonally across the room from us. Punditt's welcome address was being held in a conference room right across the hall. We had a decent view of anyone who would head to the bar after the conference, but the only way we'd be spotted was if someone came looking for us.

A very well-dressed waiter approached our table, and took our order in such a professional manner that I was almost intimidated to choose an entrée. By good providence, I was able to overcome my fears, however, and within a short time, I was feasting quite happily on a Mako shark fillet, surrounded by asparagus stalks and brown Cajun rice. Everett ordered a bottle of wine which he said was designed specially to go with a meal of fish, but as wine has a habit of putting me right to sleep, I brazenly declined, striving to maintain a professional demeanor for the rest of the evening. I had hopes of reaching marginal success.

Just before nine o'clock, the doors to the conference rooms opened, and like cattle, Punditt's mighty parishioners came flooding into the ballroom. Nicole was right. The air in the bar area crackled with an electricity of arrogance and power. Sitting back to enjoy the unfolding show, we were treated to Animal Kingdom: The Human Version. The patrons arriving now were of an entirely different stratum on the social scale. They didn't clamor for drinks; instead, they used the bar to clamor for the best opportunity to display a gold bracelet, or diamond cufflinks, or an Italian suit. People were shaking hands and smiling into one another's faces, but even from a distance, it was apparent that these people were using the opportunity to size up the competition from the world outside. It was not a coincidence that these were the people who just happened to all be involved together with Abraham Punditt. If I could find out why they all happened to be involved, then I would almost start feeling somewhat competent.

Seeing how this wasn't the most opportune time to start a counseling session with Nicole about failure issues, I settled for the next best thing, which happened to be Lil in a sequined evening gown.

"Anybody want a drink?" I asked.

"Our wine bottle has been depleted," Everett announced.

"Feel like wandering up to the bar?" I asked Lil.

"We have a waiter."

"He only brings food. Your talents are better suited for, ah, reconnaissance."

"Your wish is my command, O master," she said as she rose up lazily out of her chair.

"How come you only say that when we're surrounded by people in a public place?"

But she was already gone.

Lil's dress was cut so it showed just a bit too much of everything in all the right places. Watching her walk in it was an exercise in itself, and the closer she got to the crowd, the more she dramatized her walk. Old habits die hard.

The crowd seemed to part for her like she was Moses as she approached the bar, and it wasn't long before she held a drink in her hand that I would bet vital parts of my anatomy she didn't pay for. From where we were seated, she seemed to have the attention of two gentlemen, one a broad-shouldered older man in a three-piece suit complete with pinky ring, and the other considerably shorter and younger, wearing a flashy sport coat with his shirt opened at the collar, and dark hair that was slicked back with so much gel it stayed still when the rest of his head turned.

Lil stayed put to hear a story or two, and then smiled politely and excused herself to the opposite side of the bar. Here she placed herself back in a corner, taking in the scenery, and within five minutes was engaged in conversation with three men who happened to saunter over. Her drink was replenished, and by the time it was half empty, she slid away from her captive audience and maneuvered her way back to our table.

"You didn't get us drinks."

"No, but I did get invited to lunch tomorrow with a senator from Massachusetts, as well as asked to attend a party next month on the yacht of the governor of Connecticut."

"We should be flattered you returned to our paltry little table."

"I only returned to retrieve Nicole."

"Of course."

"I like yachts," stated Nicole.

"Before the two of you run off with the holy masses over there, did you happen to get anything that would be of use to us?"

"You're dealing with a major assemblage of assholes, but not just your ordinary, run-of-the-mill slobs. We have, converged at this conference, a collection of some major league, state-of-the-art, upper, upper echelon dickheads of the highest quality. There are lawyers, senators, congressmen, corporate presidents, and even one potential presidential nominee. With these people all in the room at the same time, I'm not sure how some of the Northeast is still operating."

"Is this the entire conference?"

"Just a faction. And don't be fooled. You have many less prominent people in attendance as well. But with some of the celebrity moguls on the who's who list, your man Punditt has some deep connections."

Lil crossed her legs and finished her drink.

"Now look over my left shoulder at the table nearest the entrance and tell me if that blond is your friend the psychotic kewpie doll."

I looked past Lil at the table in question. There, surrounded by three men, was indeed, Mrs. Lindsey Norman-Oakes.

"I'm guessing by 'psychotic' you mean the one with her head still attached."

Everett followed my gaze. "For what reason do you think she is engaging in conversation with the three gentlemen at her table?"

"Probably interviewing them for a follow-up reunion issue of *Classic* magazine."

Our waiter returned. I ordered another round of drinks and charged it to Everett's room.

"I assume this means we're not done here yet?" Lil asked.

"Hell no. We finally caught up with someone I recognize."

"So what do we do?"

"We sit here and drink our drinks and watch what happens."

"It's inspiring working with such a professional."

We sat there and drank our drinks and watched Lindsey laugh and drink and drink and laugh and touch the three men at her table at every convenience she could. A light touch of the hand, a pat on the knee; in fact, to my trained investigative eye, it looked as if Mrs. Norman-Oakes was flirting. With all three.

"Think she's spreading Christian love?"

"Rate she's going, she'll be spreading much more than that."

One gentleman left the table, and before his seat could be pushed in, another took his spot. Lindsey held court continuously, smiling, petting, caressing, and apparently winning the affections of any male who came within her grasp. This could have gone on all night, had it not been for the arrival of her husband Lawrence.

His arrival carried with it all the grace of fingernails dragging down a chalkboard. One minute, everyone was in festive spirits, and then all of a sudden, he was there. You felt like you were watching the parent drop a rock into Charlie Brown's trick-or-treat bag, and then holding your breath to see if that rock would explode.

Lindsey didn't seem to care. She kissed each of her would-be consorts good night, and stood up to kiss Lawrence. Lawrence was a bit taller than she, and Lindsey had to stand on her tiptoes to reach him. Her skirt was already too short, and the way it accompanied her body as she stretched toward Oakes was not an altogether enjoyable sight. Still, all the guys at the table seemed to really like her. Maybe she just possessed great conversational skills.

"Is that Lawrence?" Lil asked, leaning back in her chair as if she were about to take a nap.

I nodded.

"He's a big one," Nicole murmured.

"He's not that big, honey."

Nicole looked at Lil for a moment.

Lil winked. "Years of practice."

"It might be advantageous to discern his lodging in this hotel."

Everett's eyes had been scanning the room since Lawrence's entrance. Finding nothing out of the ordinary, he returned his attention to the four of us.

"I'm on it," Nicole said, and sprung up out of her seat. Before we could say anything, Oakes and Lindsey were leaving the bar, and Nicole was leaving with them.

"Kind of quick for someone so small," I said to Everett.

"You don't even know."

Lindsey's exit seemed to herald the end of the party, and after she left, the rest of the conference crowd thinned out in a rapid manner. What had minutes ago been a thriving carnival of dedicated drinkers emptied out, and the staff was left to tend to a barren regime of late-night stragglers more intent on comparing stock averages than replenishing half-filled glasses. Seeing that the most lucrative part of the night was over, the bar called last call and started cleaning up. As the house lights came up, Nicole came back to the table.

"The lovely couple is staying in room 1406," she said, picking up her purse.

"They see you?"

"I would think so. I got in the elevator with them and then stood around looking confused while I watched them go to their room on the fourteenth floor. But they have no reason to think

I'm anything important. And they were too lost in conversation with each other to pay me much attention anyway."

"You hear what they were saying?"

"No, but their body language was very loud. They spoke close together. Their tones weren't hushed, but they were quiet and very direct with each other. I couldn't tell if they were mad or just blunt with each other."

"Lindsey's conduct could warrant a little bit of both I would imagine."

"Maybe. But whatever they were doing, they weren't fighting."

We left as a tall man with a ponytail was bringing a mop and bucket over to the far end of the room and began swishing the mop back and forth in a methodical manner. We rode the elevator up to the tenth floor and got out. The hotel was very quiet. For a conference of such size, no one seemed to be making any noise after hours. At least not on our floor.

Everett and Nicole went into their room, and Lil opened the door to ours. I was not very adroit with keys, especially of the electronic kind, and it was an unspoken understanding that unless the door needed to be broken down or jimmied open, Lil was to take care of garnering access to all areas.

Everett had done a very thorough search of both rooms before we arrived, and had found one electronic bug in each of our rooms; one right underneath the radiator grille, and the other at the base of the bed's headboard against the wall. It didn't surprise me that he had found them, but it did make me curious.

There was a note that had been shoved under the door from Jacob Bollock saying that he had missed us at the introductory ceremony, and hoped to see us at breakfast. Other than that, everything was exactly as we had left it. Nothing had been touched or rifled through. Feeling content, and almost competent with the way the evening went, we undressed, turned off the lights, and went to bed.

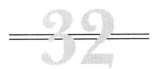

The next morning passed agonizingly slowly. As Everett and I were well known to both Punditt and Oakes, it had been decided that Nicole and Lil would attend the morning sessions and gather any information that seemed to be halfway relevant. Needless to say, this was met with less than genuine enthusiasm from the girls, but by nine thirty I was convinced they had gotten the better part of the deal.

Thanks to the added benefit of extra channels piped in by the hotel, I reached my saturation point of daytime television within fifteen minutes. I hadn't brought any books, and I wasn't smart enough to play solitaire. That left talking with Everett, but I'd have to do that later in the day anyway, and I figured I needed to conserve my strength.

I didn't take Lawrence Oakes for much of a conference attendee, and bet that if he was anywhere in the hotel, he'd probably be at the gym. The fact that he could be in there basically cut out the option of the gym for me, but if I stayed in here any longer, I'd start shooting bullets into the ceiling just out of boredom. I pulled on a T-shirt and a pair of sweatpants and left my hotel room. I took the stairwell down to a back exit and walked out into the blinding sunlight of downtown Providence.

The Westin Hotel was located at the base of a small hill. As a matter of fact, all of downtown Providence was relatively small. I had grown up in Boston, and comparatively speaking, Providence seemed like a mere three-block radius in any direction.

I started out at a slow jog and ran up the hill away from the hotel. The Providence Mall was a mammoth structure for what seemed to be a small city, and stretched the length of more than half the hill. I crested the top of the hill, turned right, and ran alongside the statehouse. Providence's statehouse was a very dignified structure, the type of architecture that invited regal splendor without any sort of pompous demeanor. It almost welcomed you simply by being there. Further down the road was the train station, and bearing right after that, I headed back down into the heart of the city, where I wound my way back to the main thoroughfare and ended up back at the hotel.

It was a small loop, but as I didn't know the city, I wanted to stay relatively close, so I decided to run intervals, speeding up on the hills, and slowing to a more moderate pace on the flat areas. As I went through my workout, I noticed the number of restaurants that were housed solely in the area in which I was confining my run. I reassessed my initial impression of the city, and decided that while it was indeed small, it seemed to have more than its share of fine dining and other various eating establishments. Providence might actually be worth a night out or two.

I ran my loop four times. It wasn't my most strenuous morning of exercise, but it got me out of my room and woke me up. That had to count for something. The lobby was sparsely populated when I entered the hotel, and I opened the door to the fire stairs and climbed ten flights back up to my room. I turned on the water and took a long, hot shower, and when I stepped back into the room, Lil was lying on the bed, wearing a less-than-cheerful face.

"You are not making me attend another session with those people."

She flipped mindlessly through the television channels using the remote.

"Not making friends?"

"I have a feeling I could make a lot of friends if I wanted to. I've never met such a group of lecherous has-beens in one concentrated area."

"Coming from you, that statement carries a lot of weight."

Lil continued to press the remote, cycling through the channels twice, and then turned off the TV.

"You can't just up and quit. What if I still need you?"

She sat up and looked at me with a blank stare.

"I assume that question is rhetorical."

Lil was dressed simply in a silk buttoned blouse and a pair of slacks. She stretched and then carefully smoothed out her blouse and crossed her feet at the ankles.

"So, you going to ask me about the conference?"

"I was going to, but then I got scared."

"Smart boy. There were four different workshops this morning. Nicole attended one entitled 'Peace and Joy, the Reward of the Calling' and I sat through 'Holding Hands Toward the Future.' Punditt visited each of them, smiling like a politician who just got laid."

Lil didn't waste much time describing the workshops, but basically it seemed that the premise of both workshops was part pep rally for giving time and money to Punditt, and part statistical analysis of where the cash and labor went. Of course, all of this was communicated through a sugary, feel-good delivery that was supposed to get the crowd sufficiently blinded by rah-rah and cheers. Luckily, Lil was not swayed by rah-rah.

The second workshop was scheduled to begin at twelve thirty, after the crowd had enjoyed an hour lunch. Lil suggested an alternate and more constructive way to spend the afternoon, and at twelve fifty-five, we were exiting the elevator on the fourteenth floor and walking down the hall to room 1406. Lil rapped hard on the door twice, and when there was no answer from within, she hunched down at eye level with the electronic lock and set to work. I stood with my back to her, scanning the hallway for anyone stupid enough to still be here.

"I thought those things were supposed to be criminal-proof," I said while she worked the lock.

"They are. I'm not a criminal."

"Did you attend classes on how to gain illegal entry?"

She ignored me and concentrated on the door.

"You forget who you're dealing with. I've had to gain access to more than one hotel room in my day. This was simply on-the-job training."

"It's proving to be a useful skill."

"I'd try to teach you, but you'd be too busy looking down my blouse."

She stood up, twisted the knob, and we walked in. The room was not as empty as we expected. A naked, hefty man was sprawled on his back on Lawrence Oakes's bed, and this gentleman was definitely not Lawrence Oakes. Straddling him and working her body like an overexerted piston was a very naked, very definite Mrs. Lindsey Oakes.

This looked like it could become interesting.

I shut the door and leaned against the wall. Lindsey stopped in mid-hump and stared at me. It took the gentleman about half a minute to realize he was the only one still working at the previous endeavor, and then he too looked over in my direction. Beads of sweat had formed on his balding head, and a smile did not seem to break through his salt-and-pepper beard. Lil walked into the room, rummaged around a bit, and found a robe which she draped over Lindsey's shoulders.

"Put this on, darling. We could be here for a while."

Lindsey absently pulled the robe around her, dismounted the gentleman, and sat herself down in one of the chairs by the bed. Her eyes never left me. The gentleman sighed, rolled over, and grabbed his jacket, which had been draped on one of the other chairs, and produced a checkbook.

"I didn't think you people did personal drive-bys," he said as he flipped through to find the next blank check in his registry. He rolled back over on his side, rested his chin in his hand, and tried to look as businesslike as a large man in his fifties who had just been caught in sexual congress with a married woman could. The fact that he was still unalterably naked did not help him achieve much success in this enterprise.

"How much do I owe you?" he said, looking straight at me. "I didn't see any camera, but I never do with you people. I assume you got something tangible, so here. I'm making this out for the same amount as last time, and you still get my regular donations at the regular intervals."

He handed me a check made out to *Search for Salvation*. The amount was enough for a weekend stay in Paris. He rolled off the bed and started pulling his pants on, muttering something about how Eve should have never grabbed Adam's cock in the first place.

Lil, meanwhile, had busied herself with rifling through Lindsey's belongings, opening drawers, searching suitcases, and so forth. This seemed to snap Lindsey out of her stupor, and she stammered over to Lil a very eloquent, "You can't do that!" a statement made even less assertive as it was exclaimed by Lindsey while she remained seated in her chair and seemed to be trying to shrink back into it as much as possible.

"Oh I most certainly can, sweetie," Lil said as she continued her search. "You see, the sooner he finds something that enables him to understand what exactly is going on here, the sooner we can leave this abominable conference. That, in turn, will allow me to salvage what remains of my vacation, and enjoy it in a much more productive manner."

"I thought it was *our* vacation."

"But," Lil continued, looking over her shoulder back at Lindsey, "feel free to call the police if you think it would help."

Lindsey pulled her knees up to her chin and hugged herself tightly. Her former companion finished adjusting his tie in the mirror, and headed for the door. I opened it for him and made a show of pocketing his check.

Lil pulled a suitcase out from the closet and opened it on the bed. She looked through it briefly and then beckoned me over.

"This might work for you."

I pulled myself off the wall and walked over to Lil. Lindsey's mouth was closed in a very tight line. I looked over Lil's shoulder. The suitcase was full of 8 x 10 photographs capturing various people in an assortment of what could come to be construed as scandalous acts. Some were blatant: sex and drug use, others were less so: a man and woman entering a hotel room, suitcases being exchanged in alleyways. The shots weren't taken by any professional, but they were clear enough. And I was pretty sure each picture was worth more than a thousand words.

"What a coincidence," I said to Lindsey. "Many of the people in these pictures are attending this very conference. Does *Search for Salvation* specialize in personal redemption as well, or does it stop with good old-fashioned blackmail?"

Lindsey gave me a look that would melt ice.

"Get out of my room," she spat.

"We could get this one framed," Lil said, holding up a photo. "And this one is very tastefully done in black and white. It could go in the kitchen."

"You're holding it upside down."

Lindsey shifted in her seat and looked as if she was ready to claw out our eyes.

"Help me out here, Lindsey. We've got you banging another guy, which, having met your husband, doesn't exactly make it distasteful. Still, I'm eighty percent sure he wouldn't like it if he found out. Two, we've got a load of incriminating evidence on Punditt's Platoon courtesy of you. I don't think he'd like this public knowledge either. Give us something to use and we'll take a walk. I swear."

"Are you trying to blackmail me?" she smirked.

"Kind of ironic."

"All you've got is a load of pictures. Which, if you take them with you, you can't prove they were ever mine. You don't have anything on me. You're out of luck…. sweetie."

I looked at Lil. She shrugged.

"OK," I said.

Lil shut the suitcase and we took it with us as we left the room.

"So what exactly do we have here?" Lil asked as we got in the elevator.

"A box full of porn."

"Great. And here I thought we might actually have something big."

"What we have here, babe, is pretty strong evidence that the Oakeses are blackmailing a majority of Punditt's mouseketeers. And I'd say it's a safe bet that Punditt is in on it somehow as well."

"Goddamn. That almost sounds like a clue."

Lil was probably right, but it had been so long since I'd seen one, I didn't want to look ignorant, so I kept my mouth shut. We got off on our floor and carried the box of photos in from our room through the adjoining door into Everett and Nicole's.

"Got us some clues," I said, dropping the box on the bed.

Nicole came over and started looking through.

"Oh, yuck," she said, stopping on the third photo.

Everett was seated at the table by the window with a stack of magazines. He closed the one he was reading and looked up.

"I couldn't find you earlier. I took a walk to the Providence Public Library and checked out as many back issues of *Classic* as I could."

Lil settled into the second chair and started leafing through an issue.

"As we had no tangible leads, and I was going to be relatively sedentary for the morning, I thought it might be one more place to garner background information. On the surface, it appears to be like any other celebrity magazine you'd find on a newsstand. However..." He pulled a copy out from the bottom of the pile. "This one might be of particular interest."

I looked at the cover. The headline across the bottom border read "Prominent Rhode Island Attorneys Linked in Scandal – Details Inside." This was the issue that started the ball rolling toward her magazine's bankruptcy.

"After reading the article, I took a second look through the program of events for this conference. The last eight pages list the major contributors to Punditt's campaign. Two of the names listed are two of the lawyers Lindsey tried to out in a scandal in that issue."

"Is there a picture of them in the magazine?"

Everett showed me the candids in *Classic* magazine of the men accused by Lindsey. I started leafing through the photos that were in the box. After about forty minutes of searching, I found a match.

Bernard Ottwain, a large, ruddy-faced lawyer with longish hair and a cowlick up front was shown handing over a briefcase to one of two gentlemen. The other fellow, with slicked-back hair to his shoulders and dressed in a sport coat and slacks, with jewelry showing at every opportunity, was handing Ottwain what looked like a large package of cocaine. Of course, I could be making an incorrect assumption. He could've been buying bags of flour wholesale.

There was a second photo paper clipped to the first, showing Ottwain through a window in his office sitting at his desk and snorting said cocaine. Both shots were obviously taken with a telephoto lens, and from the quality, were taken by someone who knew what he or she was doing.

"Someone's done their homework," I said, looking at Everett.

"Repeatedly," he said, gesturing toward the box.

I recounted the show we were treated to in Lindsey's room. It appeared we had stumbled onto an elaborate blackmail scheme. Lindsey's initial comment was correct. Technically, we didn't have anything that would prove anybody's involvement. But Punditt's devotees were now being seen in a much clearer comprehension. Things were starting to make sense. And what was in our possession was a major link to the funds that were pouring into Abraham's little piece of heaven. We had the opportunity now to start pushing some people's buttons.

I looked at the girls.

"What's Punditt got on schedule for tonight?"

"The main dinner. He's holding it at the Convention Center next to the hotel. It's the gala event of the conference. He's giving his keynote address."

Every once in a while, something fell my way.

"What time does it start?"

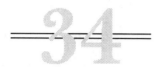

Restaurant people are good people. They're hard-working. They can fight and laugh with each other simultaneously and not miss a beat. They can set the mood of the entire room, event, or meal. They're blunt, they're honest, and the more stressful the situation, the harder they work. They'll work when everyone else parties, but they can do more damage in three hours on a Tuesday night than most people do all weekend. Most importantly, they know the meaning of a buck.

It was this last quality that enabled me to go after Punditt. I didn't have any hard evidence on him, but I figured if I pushed in the right places, I'd make him come to me. And then he'd slip up.

The dinner at the Convention Center didn't start until eight P.M., but the caterers were setting up the ballroom at five. I wandered over and got the layout of the place. The head table was set deep at the front of the room, where Punditt would be seated with other dignitaries. From the back, it looked like a reenactment of Da Vinci's *The Last Supper.* His table was long and rectangular, while the rest of the tables set around the room were the standard round shape with eight place settings each. A podium stood behind the head table, and an immense screen hung off to the side of the room, probably for showing slides or movies later in the dinner.

I found the waitress who was handling Punditt's table and introduced myself. I explained that I was an associate of Abraham's and we had a recurring competition to engage in practical jokes at all of these conferences. I gave her twenty bucks and a manila envelope, asking her to serve Abraham his meal with the envelope atop his main course. She smiled and took the envelope in her hand.

"Well, what's all the work worth if you can't have a little fun too, right?" she laughed.

"I can't wait to see his face," I smiled.

I turned and walked out the door back to my hotel room.

You could hear the noise as soon as you stepped off the escalator. We walked down the concourse to the ballroom, and the muffled rumble of the crowd grew to an imposing roar. There were a few stragglers hanging around outside the doorway as we approached, but the rest of the crowd was milling around inside. As we entered, I had to tip my hat to our Reverend Punditt. I had caught glimpses of factions of his followers here and there throughout the conference, but this was the first time I was privy to the entire group *en masse*. I had to admit it was almost a respectable sight.

The ballroom was filled to capacity, and I'm sure I wasn't fully aware of the magnitude of the power that was rubbing elbows together in here. I was fully aware that I didn't care.

We stepped deeper into the room, and I searched the crowd for Punditt. It was a challenge looking for him amid the ties, skirts, and cufflinks swimming through the room, but I finally locked on him about three-quarters of the way into the room. He was dressed in a striking olive suit replete with a tie clip that sparkled across the floor and into the foyer. His hair was freshly cut and looked as if it had been styled earlier in the day, and I'm sure I would be able to see the reflection of the Holy Ghost in the shine on his shoes. Even if we weren't enmeshed in the crowd of suits at the door, I doubt Punditt would have seen us. He was too busy shaking hands and smiling enthusiastically with everyone he came upon as he made his way to his table.

Abraham took his seat at the head table, and the announcement was made that dinner would be served. We took our seats at our table, which was situated in the middle of the room and off to the side by an exit. At least our status was high enough that we didn't merit the table by the kitchen door.

Everyone took their time getting to their seats, but eventually everyone was seated, at which point Punditt stood up to say grace. He had a microphone standing at a podium next to his table, and as he spoke the blessing, everyone bowed their heads in unison. Punditt returned to his seat and the caterers began to bring out the meals.

As with most socialite occasions, dinner consisted of a selection of courses, and the wait staff busied themselves with bringing out the first round, which was a small salad accompanied by a cup of soup. This part of the meal was up to par with most other catered fare, which meant I contented myself with the dinner rolls while waiting for the main entrée.

It took quite awhile to service the entire crowd, but the wait staff was very efficient, and split the duties so that half of them had the salad plates cleared while the other half began bringing out the main course. I looked for my waitress up front, and sure enough, she was delivering Abraham's meal complete with my discreet piece of mail. She leaned in and whispered something in his ear as she placed his plate in front of him, and the two of them shared a brief chuckle. She walked away to service her other patrons, and Punditt opened the manila envelope.

I had chosen the picture very carefully, and had complimented myself on the tastefulness of the black and white depiction of an older gentleman and two younger women engaging in some lewd sexual acts. Punditt pulled out the photo, and from his reaction, one might think he was looking at a picture of his grandmother's eighty-fifth birthday. But if you were looking for it like I was, you saw a momentary flinch when he initially saw the shot, and his face flushed briefly when he realized where the picture came from.

His eyes dove into his audience, searching for the messenger who had sent the envelope to him. He scanned through the crowd, but there was no way he was going to notice me amidst everyone seated and eating, so I did what any rational human being would do. I stood up. And waved. Vigorously. Punditt looked over at me, and a wave of recognition passed over his face as our eyes locked. I'm sure the smirk I sent in his direction wreaked havoc with his digestion, but the meal hadn't been that good to begin with.

I stopped waving, and very slowly and methodically, I began to clap. One by one, people at other tables stood up and joined in the clapping, and within minutes, the entire congregation was on their feet, giving Punditt a standing ovation. Punditt had no choice but to acknowledge the applause with a gracious nod. I gave him my full Cheshire grin, to which he returned a baleful glare. Everyone slowly returned to their seats, and the dessert carts were brought out.

Abraham was stuck. He was the main event tonight, which meant he couldn't very well leave. I, on the other hand, could get up and walk out at a moment's notice. I had the drop on him, and he knew it. He had no way of knowing what I was going to do, where I was going to go, or who I was going to talk to. I'm sure his imagination was in overdrive right now.

The caterers came through, clearing the tables and bringing coffee. The crowd settled back in their seats as Abraham got up and began his speech. I toasted him with my water glass as he stood at the podium. Once he was fifteen minutes into his talk, I stood up, excused myself from the table, and holding my head high, walked across the room and out the main door.

I'm pretty sure he saw me leave.

Lil met me ten minutes later in the hotel lobby, and we took the elevator up to the penthouse. Punditt had rented the suite for himself during his stay. Why give to charity when you could live in luxury for the weekend?

We walked halfway down the hall to the door of the suite. I watched the elevator while Lil kneeled down and worked her magic on the lock. I had issues opening the door using the damn key; there was no way I'd ever learn how to pick these locks. Lil stood up, cracked the door open, and gave me a kiss on the forehead. Then she turned, walked back to the elevator, got in, and left me alone.

I stepped into the penthouse suite and closed the door behind me. Abraham certainly didn't have a problem spending his church's money for his lodgings. His suite was a miniature palace. Without exaggeration, it took up over half of the entire twentieth floor of the hotel. I walked through an antechamber that housed a couple closets, and entered the mainstay of the apartment.

The apartment was circular in design, and three quarters of the walls were sheer glass windows that ran from ceiling to floor, and overlooked the city streets below. To my right was a formal dining area, complete with a mahogany table and eight ornate chairs. Past that was the actual kitchen, and to my left was a thoroughfare that led to a bathroom that looked as if it had been done entirely in marble.

Directly in front of me was a resplendent living room which contained furnishings that harkened back to days when each individual piece of furniture was made to order. I stood in back of a large white sofa, and facing me were three chairs that all looked as if someone should be sitting in one of them wearing a silk robe, smoking a pipe, and reading Charles Dickens. An overly elaborate glass tabletop was in the middle of the room, and if I dared to look, I'm sure I would have found the leg fixtures to be made of gold, and probably resembling talons from some sort of bird.

Walking through the living room, I came to a staircase that led down to Punditt's bedroom. The bedroom was ten stairs deeper than the rest of the apartment, and the steepness of the staircase gave the illusion of privacy from the rest of the suite. I climbed down the stairs and found a neatly made up king sized bed, a nine-drawer bureau with an extra-large vanity mirror, and an upright cedar chest which housed four separate units to hang all his clothes. Two of the units contained a wide array of sport coats and slacks, but the final two were steadfastly locked. If Punditt didn't show up relatively soon, that would give me a project to work on.

I climbed back up the stairs into the living room. There were two lamps sitting on end tables by each of the outside chairs, and a large upright lamp hovered over the sofa. All of these were turned off. The blinds were open, and outside lights from nearby buildings as well as the hotel itself cast an eerie glow through the giant windows. I searched every drawer and cabinet in the apartment, but didn't find any gun or weapon Abraham might be keeping. Of course I couldn't account for the locked drawers downstairs.

A full-size upright mirror stood in one corner of the living room, and I stopped to admire myself in it. Not seeing anything particularly attractive in my reflection, I chose one of the armchairs, sat down, and awaited the return of Abraham Punditt.

I didn't think it would take him long to come back to his room. I had to hand it to him. When push came to shove, he stepped up to the plate. He knew I had let him see me for a reason, and he also had to have a pretty good idea that I'd be waiting for him somewhere in the vicinity when he got back.

But he still put on the performance of a lifetime during his Saturday night special. I should've been surprised, but I wasn't. I was pretty sure Abraham Punditt was capable of a lot more things than he let on.

I heard footsteps approaching the door. It didn't take great detective work to discern that it was Punditt. This was the only room on the floor. I heard the key being inserted into the lock. The knob twisted and the door opened. Only the figure who stepped in wasn't Abraham Punditt. It was Lawrence Oakes.

Some detective.

He closed the door and walked into the foyer. He peered into the light and shadows that played across the living room and found my eyes. He walked in a little further and was cloaked in a red haze from one of the neon lights outside. I didn't know if he had come here looking for Punditt or come here expecting to find me. I didn't ask. I was sure I wasn't going to like the answer regardless.

"You couldn't leave well enough alone, could you?" The sound cut across the room with a crispness of purpose that matched his walk. "You had to keep nosing around."

"Actually, Mister Oakes, I tried to ignore this thing in every possible way. You people keep sucking me back in. I've been threatened, beat up, held at gunpoint, and had dead bodies dropped on my doorstep. I'm simply sick of being pushed around."

"Walk away now." He spread his hands like a minister absolving me of guilt. "You'll never hear from us again. All will be forgotten. You have my word."

I shook my head.

"I'm not that stupid, sir. Besides, you're missing the point."

He stared at me in silence.

"You went after Lil, Lawrence."

He stood directly in front of me. I was still sitting. My hands were clasped in front of me in perfect repose. I made no effort to get up.

"You shouldn't have done that. She wasn't involved at all. You let me down. I would've thought if you wanted me, you'd be man enough to come after me yourself."

To his credit, he remained calm. He didn't move at all from where he stood.

"I'm here now." His voice crunched like freshly laid gravel.

"That you are, Larry. And to show you what a sport I am, I'll even let you throw the first punch."

He made a sound that could've been mistaken for a laugh in a dead man's body.

"Skinny fuck like you? That's not sporting, pal, that's patronizing."

I smiled back at him.

"You don't realize how big this thing is." His eyes narrowed. "And the lengths I'm willing to go to keep it." He smiled down at me from where he stood. "I suppose you're gonna tell me you'll win 'cause you're the good guy, right?"

"That's where you're wrong, Larry." I stopped smiling. "I'm not a good guy."

"Neither am I."

He lunged forward and pulled me up by my shirtfront. I drove my knee up but he twisted his hip and blocked his groin. He was fast. He landed a hard punch across my face and then rocked my skull with an uppercut that sent me sprawling back over the armchair. I crashed into the end table, and the lamp smashed onto the floor.

Oakes came charging after me and kicked his boot into my midsection. I rolled away from his follow-up and grabbed a leg from the broken table. I swung it into his shin, which slowed him down enough for me to scramble to my feet. I drove the leg down on his head and then smashed his nose with it. That was enough to bring him to his knees, but he reached out blindly and grabbed my arm. He pulled me toward him, and instead of fighting him, I went forward willingly. The extra momentum caused him to fall backwards, and I landed on top of him. I buried four punches in his face, causing him to spit blood but no teeth. I wasn't as strong as I'd like. I jerked my knee into his jaw, and then pushed myself off his body.

The upright mirror was standing in back of him. I took hold of the top of the wooden frame and pulled the mirror down on top of him. The glass shattered onto his face. His body convulsed involuntarily in pain. Oakes pulled the mirror off of him and stood up. He turned in a half-circle to his left. He held the wooden frame in his hands in front of him. He tried to yell, but the only sound that came out was a gurgle from deep in his throat that sounded like a muffled growl.

Blood and glass covered his face. Between that and his rage, he was half blind. He couldn't see me, and he didn't know where he was. He was a big man, and he was angry. He raised the wooden frame and what was left of the mirror over his head, as if to strike out in my direction. That's when he felt it. The shift in weight as he held the frame over his head made him take an involuntary step back. Only there was nothing in back of him. He was at the top of the stairs over Punditt's bedroom. He stepped out into space. The mirror fell from his hands and landed below him with a crash. For a moment, he looked like a cartoon character, one foot on the ground, one foot in the air, arms spinning wildly, trying to keep his balance. I could have reached out and grabbed him. Everett would probably say I should have.

He bounced off two stairs before he hit the floor. I stood on the ledge and looked down at his broken body below. The lights from outside illuminated him in a grotesque manner. One eye still stared out at the living world. If I thought he deserved the dignity, I would have shut it.

"I told you you'd only get the first punch."

Lil came back into our room and poured another bucket of ice onto my swollen hand.

"So how long did the fight last?"

"Altogether? A total of five minutes."

She sighed.

"You never were much of a fighter."

"I'm still alive, sweetheart. Who's lying at the bottom of the stairs with a broken neck?"

"'Persistent' is much different than 'good fighter.'" She rubbed a cotton swab coated in a thick jelly over the mass that was formerly my right eye. "What shall we do about the body?"

"Leave it. Let Punditt find it. Consider it a gift in return for the one left on our porch."

"And just chalk it up to coincidence when your friend Sergeant Simon comes calling and sees you in this condition?"

"I'll tell her my girlfriend beats me. She'll probably buy you a beer."

My whole body hurt. It wasn't the good ache of working your body, but the dead, lumpy feeling of having your body worked over. I wasn't tired, but I was dull. I sat in the armchair in our room and looked out the window at nothing in particular.

"What time is it?"

"Quarter of eleven."

"How long did Punditt speak?"

"His speech lasted about an hour, almost until ten. But he's still down there holding a question-and-answer forum. We left, but a good amount of people looked like they were going to stay."

"Even if they weren't, he'd come up with something. He thinks he's giving Oakes time to work me over and get rid of my body."

"You think Punditt sent him over and not Lindsey?"

"Doesn't matter. It's the same thing."

Talking didn't hurt as much as I thought it would. I was either getting stronger or getting used to being hit.

"I'll go tell Nicole and Everett to start packing. You find a house phone on another floor and call the front desk telling them you heard yelling and a fight coming from Punditt's room. Tell them to send security immediately."

"You like giving orders. I take it we're leaving?"

"Yep. We've rattled Punditt a couple times. Now he's gonna be tied up with the police. That'll give us some breathing room to figure out what to do next."

"Don't you think your name will be one he tosses out to the police first?"

"Maybe. But if he does, he's limited. Why would I be in his room? We're not even registered under our real names here."

"All right. I'll go make the phone call. Give me ten minutes."

"Try to sound like a damsel in distress."

"Don't push it."

Lil left the room. I pulled my gym bag out of the closet and then went next door to get Nicole and Everett.

We were home at the cottage for two days before Sergeant Simon asked to see me. I was the only one home when she called. Nicole and Lil were at the beach, Everett was out being academic, and I was drinking my first gin and tonic of the day while reading a book I'd brought with me on Howlin' Wolf. Once in a while, I alternated and read the label on the gin bottle just for diversity.

"Your friend Abraham Punditt is making quite a name for himself lately," she said when I picked up the phone.

"He's not my friend."

"That's the first thing you've said that's almost made me like you. How about you and your associate Mister Jones come down and see me for a minute so we can discuss Punditt's life and compare notes on how much of it he seems likely to have left?"

"Miss Simon, don't you think I see through your little charade of using Punditt just to get a chance to see me again?"

"You're not funny."

"You've said that before. What makes you think I know or care anything about Abraham Punditt?"

"What makes you think I won't send a squad car out to pick you up and haul you in here personally if you don't get your ass down here in the next hour?"

With that, she hung up and I was left talking to a dial tone. The cottage was clean, it was Lil's turn to cook dinner, and the only thing I planned on actively pursuing for the rest of the day was getting more ice for my glass. I might as well get this over with. I stretched, stood up, found my shoes, and put on my sunglasses. I looked around the living room once and grunted. This was the first break I'd had in a while to have time to myself. I was sure that somewhere in the deep recesses of her mind, Sergeant Lucille Simon knew that as well.

The police station was just as I'd left it last time, and the library next door hadn't changed either. My face had healed back to simply having a couple dark bruises, so even I didn't look much different from my last visit here. Summer in Narragansett. The icon of consistency.

Sergeant Simon was seated behind her desk filling out some paperwork. Her hair was pulled back in a ponytail, and she was wearing a cream-colored blouse and beige sport jacket. The blouse was open enough to expose a silver chain she wore around her neck, and her nails showed off a dark red polish as she signed her name to the last three documents. She looked up as I sat down. She glanced at my face and then sat back in her chair with a slight smile.

"Shiner?" she said over tented fingers.

"Barroom brawl," I replied. "I was defending three women's honor simultaneously."

"Uh-huh. Where's your partner?"

"Taking a tour of the *Providence Journal* newsroom." She stared at me. "C'mon, Lucille. I couldn't make that one up if I tried."

"Your boy Punditt is getting a lot of unwanted attention right now. Cops take it kind of personally when one of their own shows up dead in a person's room."

"He's not my boy. I don't care. And that cop was dirtier than the dreams I had about you last weekend."

"You might be right. But I thought you weren't interested."

She kept her hands tented in front of her and tapped her forefingers against her lips. I sat back in my chair and rested my arms on the armrests. We looked at each other for a while.

Finally Simon spoke. "Ok, Mister Miller, here's the deal. I have a resident of my town who keeps turning around to find dead bodies at his feet. I also have a vacationing private dick who seems to be nearby whenever one of these bodies becomes dead."

"I was nowhere near that last one."

She cleared her throat in the same manner my ninth grade teacher did when I was trying to talk my way out of a detention.

"As far as I'm concerned, you're out of your jurisdiction here. And, officially speaking, you're not even affiliated with this case. However, if anything — unofficially of course — comes your way that you think may be of particular interest to this case, I would appreciate your mentioning it to me. Are we on the same page here?"

"Officially?"

She shut her eyes, and I thought she was actually going to count to ten. But when she opened them again, I had only made it to three. She leaned forward and rested her elbows on the desk, her tented fingers now interlacing with each other.

"Why do you think Oakes was a dirty cop?"

"Just a hunch."

She nodded, more to herself than to me.

"If that hunch grows into anything substantial, please let me know."

"I will."

She picked up her stack of papers and stood. I remained sitting where I was. She looked like she thought about saying something but then decided against it. Instead she looked down at my arms.

"God, you're a hairy bastard," she said, and walked out of her office.

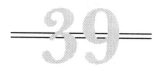

I hadn't been entirely truthful with my friend Miss Simon. Everett was not taking a tour of the *Providence Journal* newsroom when I spoke with her. Don't get me wrong, it was actually on his "things to do" list, but for the past two days, he had been searching to find Bernard Ottwain, one of the four lawyers who helped Lindsey Oakes's magazine into bankruptcy, and who, conversely, was now being blackmailed by Lindsey and Punditt. While I was having a staredown with Sergeant Simon yesterday, Everett was driving around Warwick, Rhode Island locating the precise address of Ottwain's office. And so, at nine thirty on a crisp, warm summer day, Everett and I were cruising down Post Road toward the office of Bernard Ottwain, attorney at law.

"Why do you think her demeanor has changed?" Everett asked me.

"I don't know. She wasn't hostile to me, and she almost encouraged me to continue poking around. Maybe she thinks Oakes was dirty too."

"Or maybe she's involved somehow too."

"I don't think so. Punditt has smelled bad from the start. Lucille's reaction to the first two deaths was genuine outrage. This time she almost seemed satisfied, like it was expected, or even a bonus somehow; like something fell into place."

"Or maybe we're putting things in place for her."

"There is that. But there's something about her that's legitimate."

"What?"

"She doesn't like me."

"Bright girl."

Warwick, Rhode Island is a good-sized city that is known for, among other things, housing the only airport in the state, and having a six-mile stretch of road that serves as its version of "Main Street," but goes by the name of Route 2. No such thing as overdoing it in this town. Everett and I were journeying toward the former of the two, as Ottwain's office was two traffic lights past the airport. Of course I missed the turn, and had to pull into the parking lot of a Hooters restaurant to turn around.

"We could just call it a day and stay here," I said to Everett. "Hooters girls are almost always friendly."

He shook his head.

I pulled out into traffic, veered left at the traffic light, and three blocks down pulled into the parking lot of Bernard Ottwain. His office was a modest little converted house. It had yellow shingles, brown shutters, and a sign bearing his name hanging off a signpost on the front lawn. The driveway had been enlarged to accommodate four vehicles, but there was only one car parked. I pulled in behind it, and Everett and I got out of the car.

"Lock it?"

"The top's down, Everett."

Everett picked a manila envelope off the back seat, and the two of us walked up to the front door. I opened the door, and Everett and I stepped into a small anteroom. There was a lavatory off to our right, an empty desk to our left, and three chairs seated around a table with magazines in front of us. The door beyond that was open, and a small hallway extended to a kitchenette where we heard someone rummaging around. We took two of the seats by the table and waited. Presently a woman walked down the hallway from the kitchenette into the waiting area and smiled at us.

"Good morning," she said and sat behind the reception desk by the door. "I was just putting some coffee on. Do you have an appointment with Mister Ottwain?"

"No ma'am. We were hoping we could speak with him briefly before he got busy today."

"Well, he's not in yet, but he should be in by the hour. And his first appointment isn't until eleven, so I can put you down for ten fifteen."

"That'd be great," I said.

We sat in silence for the next twenty minutes, mindlessly flipping through the magazines and newspapers scattered on the table while the receptionist organized herself for the day. Within twenty minutes, another car pulled into the driveway and Ottwain walked through the entrance. He nodded good morning at the receptionist and walked through a door behind her desk. Ten minutes after that, the phone buzzed on her desk. She spoke into it briefly, placed it back in the cradle, looked over at us, and smiled again.

"Mister Ottwain will see you now."

She held the door for us and closed it after we had entered. Ottwain's office was very well furnished. He sat at the far end of the room, behind a large mahogany desk complete with gold pens in a desk blotter. The carpeting was deep and the wall was adorned with a variety of plaques and framed certificates. A bay window next to his desk overlooked the street and let in too much sunlight. Bernard gave us a warm smile and motioned for us to sit down.

"How may I help you two gentlemen?" he asked.

Everett passed the manila envelope across the desk to him.

"We need your assistance with this," I said.

Ottwain opened the envelope and pulled out the two glossy photographs of him snorting coke in an office. His face flushed red, and he put the photographs down on the desk. He looked at us and spoke carefully in a measured tone.

"What the hell is this? I paid my dues two months ago. I'm good until November."

Bernard was a big man, and it was near impossible for him to conceal his movements. His arm was moving slowly to his right behind his desk. I pulled out my gun and leveled it at his forehead.

"Put your hands on the desk, Bernard. There's no reason to sound an alarm, nor is there any reason to attempt to shoot us."

"Says the man with the gun," Bernard said. He had stopped moving.

"Put your hands on the desk, and I'll do the same."

He did. I did. If it was any more peaceful, it could've been Christmas.

"Now do we look like the kind of losers who would associate with Abraham Punditt, let alone work for him?"

He looked genuinely confused.

"I don't get it."

I put my gun back in my holster, and picked the photos off Bernard's desk. I sat back, crossed my legs, and looked at him.

"All we want is information. We know Abraham Punditt and Lindsey and Lawrence Oakes are blackmailing you among others for inordinate amounts of money. We know that you were one of four attorneys who drove Lindsey's magazine into bankruptcy and are now being blackmailed by her. What we want to know is how Punditt and the Oakeses are pulling it off."

He chuckled.

"Uh-huh. I see. And you can just walk in here and expect that I'll cooperate with you fully and at your whim."

"Yep."

"Why on earth would I do that?"

"Because if you do, then you get to keep the pictures."

That made him perk up. The chuckling stopped.

"All right. You present a somewhat tempting offer. How do I know there aren't copies of those pictures elsewhere that will come back to bite me in the ass anyway after I give you what you want?"

"Because I give you my word. Because when it's November, nobody will come around looking for another payment. Because if you give us a straight story, the people involved in this blackmail scheme will be going away for a long time.

Because if you don't tell us what the hell is going on, my partner and I will walk out of here and paste these photos on the front page of every newspaper in the state. You don't have a helluva lot of options here, Bernie."

"All right, all right," he said, pushing the air in front of him with his hands. "Calm down, you've made your point." He let out an audible sigh. "Well, if we're going to do this, we might as well do this right."

He got up from his desk and walked across the room to a large closet. He opened the closet and returned to his desk with three glasses and a bottle of Glenlivet. He poured himself a hefty shot, and reached over to the other glasses. Everett put his hand up and I shook my head.

"Very well," he said, lifting his glass. "More for me."

He downed the shot and placed the glass back on the desktop. He leaned back in his chair and closed his eyes. When he reopened his eyes, they were very dark.

"Gentlemen," he said, "let me tell you a story."

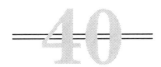

"Ever heard of Erica Gold?" Ottwain asked.

I shook my head. Everett nodded.

"How about Anthony Lucelli?"

I shook my head. Everett nodded.

If we kept this up, we could move on to patting our heads while rubbing our stomachs at the same time.

Ottwain poured himself another drink, sipped it once, and put it down. The sun streaming in from outside was in stark contrast to his mood. There should have been cigarette smoke hovering over us while he spoke in hushed tones in a dimly lit room. So much for theatre.

"If you've heard of Ms. Gold, you know she is a very prominent lawyer in the state of Rhode Island. What do you know of Mister Lucelli?"

"I know he was put away a few years ago for drug trafficking. The FBI had him pegged as one of the major suppliers on the eastern side of the country."

"Yes indeed. They put him away November of 2002 to be exact. Now do you know the connection between Ms. Gold and Anthony Lucelli?"

This time it was Everett's turn to shake his head.

A froglike grin split Ottwain's face.

"Not many do."

According to Ottwain, Erica Gold was a very, very good criminal lawyer. She was also very, very wealthy, very, very intelligent, and very, very vindictive. In short, the woman was a powerful bitch. And not in a good way. While Ottwain was talking, I matched up Lil against Erica in my head. I was pretty sure Lil could take her in three rounds until I learned that Erica had about forty pounds on Lil. Probably take Lil four rounds.

"She loved her money," Bernard continued, "and she had every reason to. She bought everything. Including her reputation."

The money Gold poured out to bribe witnesses, buy information, and keep her criminal contacts built her place in the upper stratum of Rhode Island law. However, in order for her to maintain her own status quo of that particular standing, she was driven to look for income elsewhere, not all of it always being legal. One of those forays led her to Anthony Lucelli.

Lucelli was a professor at Redd College in Providence. He taught literature, and specialized in examining everything through the gay perspective. According to Lucelli, everything ever written held subconscious ties to feelings of homosexuality and homoeroticism, and dammit, he'd show them to you whether you wanted to see them or not. Ernest Hemingway, fag; the Old Man was fishing for the little boy, not the fish. John Steinbeck, fag; George and Lennie were running from town to town holding hands. Mark Twain, fag; Tom and Huck were having their own adventures between the lines. Richard Wright, fag; Bigger Thomas killed Mary Dalton to make her boyfriend jealous.

I had long ago come to the conclusion that English professors were the con artists of education. They could access an infinite number of theories to prove whatever insights they wanted to make about any particular book. Anthony Lucelli confirmed that theory ad nauseum.

"In 1999, Anthony was arrested and brought before the courts on three counts of drug possession. Erica signed on as his attorney and got him off with three years' probation and sixty hours of community service. Then she put him to work for her."

Ottwain's voice had a pleasant rhythm to it while he was telling his tale. He might as well have been reading us *Winnie the Pooh*. I honestly thought he would fall asleep in the middle of his own story.

"Gold staged it so Anthony's community service caused him to champion gay rights. In this day of political correctness, there was no way he was going to come off looking like anything other than a hero. Redd College really didn't have anything big in the way of representation of gay students. So Lucelli went to work without even having to leave his home turf."

According to Ottwain, Lucelli spent his community service hours rallying and petitioning for gay representation on campus. And, true to form, the press ate him up. His name was plastered all over Providence. He was invited out to speak. He was invited to marches. His PR was very good, and people started to take notice of Anthony Lucelli. His reputation grew to the point where he was able to sequester a small parcel of land on the campus and, through the use of various donations, build the Gay and Lesbian Center at Redd College. All of this, of course, was in accordance with the plans of Erica Gold.

"Anthony was being directed by Erica the entire time. This building was just another step in progress. In addition to his classes, Lucelli became the director of the Gay and Lesbian Center, utilizing the building as a non-profit organization to strengthen the homosexual awareness of the Redd College community. The center ran workshops, brought in speakers, ran awareness clinics, the whole deal."

Where the general public's awareness was not as strong was in Anthony Lucelli's off-campus activities. Ms. Gold had done a thorough background check on Anthony before she decided to represent him in court. Her contacts informed her that while Lucelli had been picked up for drug possession, he was starting to get a decent grasp on the distribution angle as well. Erica saw this opportunity, and took it and ran with it.

"The center sustained its existence by garnering donations from various organizations, corporations, and philanthropists. Because this allowed it to account for a fluctuating annual income, Erica and Anthony used it as a front to launder money from Anthony's growing drug trade."

When Erica learned Anthony was a dealer as well as a user, the only thing she chastised him for was not thinking big enough. As soon as he was out of the courts, she put him in contact with people who would help attach him with a very large audience for his merchandise. The center was built, the deals started growing, and the money started rolling in.

"Erica didn't allow Anthony to be stupid. He never dealt anything himself, nor did he conduct any dealings on campus. He had runners who would carry the stuff for him, and collect his money. He worked the streets in Providence, and some schools in South County. Thanks to Erica's work, he grew a small legion of workers, while he just sat back, played master of ceremonies, and collected his cash.

"Problem was, Erica was too good. Some very big people owed her some favors, and set her up with such strong customer base that too much money was coming in. There was no way, even with the patrons and contributors they had, that they could account for the money that was going to be passing through. So Erica made some phone calls to some of her colleagues who were equally as corrupt as she, myself included, and made some offers.

"There were three of us. All we had to do was create some dummy corporations we could pass off as major contributors to Anthony at Redd College. The false donations would balance out the actual income," he paused. He took a moment and looked at us. "It really was incredibly easy. You just shuffle some papers, put a seal on them, and you have a verifiable paper trail that justifies everything."

"Until you have a semi-intelligent reporter notice that those corporations don't really exist."

"Until that," he nodded with his eyes closed. "Until that. It wasn't even Lindsey Norman who actually discovered any of the story. By that point, *Classic* magazine was so big, she had dozens of reporters working for her. We only went after her because it was her magazine, she was well-known, and we could make enough of a spectacle of her and sue her for enough money to shut her up."

"But by that point, the FBI had been showing a growing interest in you as well," Everett intoned.

"Yeah. And Anthony didn't help matters. He was sloppy. Erica couldn't watch him one hundred percent, y'know? He did things you just don't do. Liked to show off his cash every so often. Couldn't help it. Had an ego as big as a bull. But when the FBI is watching, and a college professor is showing off his Rolex, his designer clothes, his Jag....things like that start turning a lot of heads."

"And Erica isn't stupid."

"Erica isn't stupid. She knows when to cut her losses. She's smart, she can always move on to the next money venture. So she sets him up. Tells him there's a huge order of cocaine coming in. Asks him to store it in the Gay and Lesbian Center for two hours — between one thirty and three thirty in the morning — while his vendors prepare it for distribution. Anthony's not too keen on the idea, but he starts seeing dollar signs, and for him, that's the next best thing to sex.

"Erica makes a phone call, Anthony sits down to wait for his man to show up, and the next thing he knows, an onslaught of cops come barreling through his front door, and he's caught sitting with his thumb up his ass next to a small mountain of coke. Erica makes sure the right prosecutor takes the case, and ol' Anthony goes away for such a long time, they'll probably name his cell block after him."

"Arresting officer?"

"Lawrence Oakes."

"Just thought I'd ask."

"So Lucelli and Gold ran a drug operation off a college campus. Big deal. What's that got to do with Punditt and his million-dollar blackmail bonanza?"

"Patience, my dear boy, patience," Ottwain said. He pressed the fingertips of both hands together and took in a deep breath through his nose. "And don't be giving too much credit to Mister Abraham Punditt. More than one of us has played fall guy for Ms. Gold. I'm sure Abraham is hollering for a lawyer right now. Do you think anyone is answering?"

Ottwain poured himself another drink. The more he drank, the more he sounded like he was hosting *Masterpiece Theater*. Some guys start slurring when they drink, this guy starts sounding like Tony Blair.

Erica Gold knew an opportunity when she saw one. Lindsey Oakes had no concrete evidence of their operation, but she had knowledge. That either meant that Erica was careless or Lindsey was able to dig shit up. Erica opted for choice number two, because even entertaining the former was like suggesting the sun would rise in the west tomorrow.

Erica also recognized the fact that Lindsey had become a woman who was accustomed to having wealth, wealth that had just disappeared at the snap of Erica's fingers. Women who abruptly lose their wealth can be somewhat easily coerced into doing almost anything to retrieve it if they are shallow enough. Erica bet that Lindsey didn't have much more depth than a wading pool.

Lindsey was officially bankrupt on December 28, 2002. On February 24, just before the bank foreclosed on Lindsey's estate in Jamestown, Erica arrived at her door with a bottle of champagne and a proposition: help me dig up dirt on the prominently wealthy, and together we'll blackmail them and make you rich again.

Lindsey almost broke her front teeth, she was nodding so vigorously as she poured the champagne down her throat.

Gathering evidence was not to be a problem. Lawrence had access to various surveillance equipment and decent training in how to use it. Sex was a convincing bartering tool from Lindsey, as was the vision of trying to live up to her lifestyle expectations on a state trooper's salary. When it came to shallow, Lawrence didn't swim out too much farther than Lindsey in the ocean of life.

"Lucelli was in jail, Erica was removed from the dirty work, and had Lawrence and Lindsey doing it for her. The only loose ends were the three of us she had hired earlier to help create false charities."

They became the Oakeses' first assignment. Bernard was captured on film sampling some of the leftovers from Anthony Lucelli, and the second one, an attorney of fifty-some years by the name of Charles Lescoe, was caught being excessively friendly with two young Asian girls who were sixteen if he was lucky.

"Those pictures get out, we're disbarred. It's not just the job, it's the reputation. This state's small. Word travels fast. And because Rhode Island's so small, anything that is newsworthy becomes shouted over to the rest of the country."

Not everyone was blackmailable. Erica's third associate in the drug laundering, an attorney named Heather Magnate, went for a walk on Newport's Cliff Walk one crisp afternoon in late March and never returned. Her body washed up on shore two days later.

"Heather was Erica's only death that I know of. She's smart. She only wants money. Hence, she only goes after people who have something big to lose if their reputation is soiled and who can afford to pay the big bucks to keep it from getting soiled.

Although…" He looked at the manila folder I held in my hands. "That could be about to change."

"There's been a couple deaths since then."

He nodded. "Crispin. Lindsey's sister." He took a good swallow of the Glenlivet. The bottle was about half empty now. It'd been full when we arrived. "Can't help yuh there, mate." He poured himself another glass, getting just as much on his desk blotter as he did in his tumbler.

"Where does Punditt fit into all this?" He was starting to fade. I didn't want to lose him just yet.

"Punditt? Punditt's her bleedin' Anthony Lucelli." He'd be praising the queen mother after another drink. "All their money gets funneled through his Praise God organization. Oakes benched him awhile back and then kept him on a short leash to make an extra buck or two on the side. Called 'im in when this train got rollin'. Slapped a suit an' tie on 'im. Now he's Jesus."

Bernard finished the rest of his drink in a one big swallow, leaned his head back against his leather armchair, and closed his eyes. His chest moved methodically up and down. In a few minutes, he'd be snoring.

I looked at Everett.

"We get enough?"

"We're not getting any more."

I tossed the manila folder on his desk. We both got up and left the room. I pulled the door to when we were in the antechamber out front. His secretary was seated at her desk, busying herself with the pile of paperwork in front of her.

"You might want to cancel his appointments for the rest of the day," I said.

"Already did," she said without looking up.

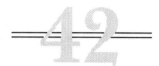

It was mid-afternoon and I was having coffee with Lucille Simon. Actually, she was drinking coffee; I was sitting across from her in a booth, nursing a glass of water. The restaurant was smaller than my kitchen. Lucille informed me that it was a bistro, and while I considered it cramped as hell, she assured me it was in actuality, cozy and warm.

The walls were cracked plaster, and the floor was the faded linoleum that I can remember running rampant in my elementary school cafeteria. Vines grew on the inside of the building, which I wasn't sure was some sort of new-wave art deco, or a testament to the questionable roofing that topped the building. A young girl dressed in all black sat at the counter by the door, the lone cash register perched in front of her. She had two metal hoops pierced through her nose, and one through her right eyebrow. She was reading a paperback book and seemed blissfully unaware of our presence. I wasn't sure if there was a kitchen on the premises, which was probably a good thing, because if I wanted some food, I would have aged three years before someone returned to take our order.

Sergeant Simon looked at me over her oversized blue coffee mug. Steam was billowing off it at such a rate that by the time we were ready to leave, there was a good chance we'd need a foghorn to find the door. It also confirmed the fact that there was no way in hell our waitress would ever find us again.

"He wasn't lying about Lucelli," she said. "I was just getting out of the academy when he was busted. Made headlines for a month."

She held her coffee cup with both hands and took a sip.

"How about Gold?"

"Tough. I don't know the full extent of her activities, but I know she hits hard. She scares the right people."

"Is Punditt scared?"

"He should be."

I could never finish a glass of water without the ice cubes rushing to the top of the glass and spilling the last swallow down the front of me. As I tilted the glass toward me, history repeated itself once again.

"Think you could get me in to see him?" I asked, drying my shirt with a cloth napkin.

"Maybe. Why?"

"He knows me. He knows I know things, but he doesn't know what. He's got no one to turn to right now. I push the right buttons, I may be able to crack his increasingly fragile psyche."

"Fragile?"

"Like glass."

Narragansett, Rhode Island is home to three types of people.
You have the disgustingly affluent, who pay a ridiculous amount
of cash to live in a chic piece of real estate on the oceanfront
and put a street name that just screams money on the return
address of their mail. You have the college kids, who take
Mommy and Daddy's money and use it to destroy a perfectly
good piece of property every year, and then try to pay their
last month's rent by recycling empty beer kegs. Lastly, you
have the normal people, who work at least two jobs and scrape
up enough money to secure a mortgage on a modest two- to
three-bedroom cottage, allowing them to keep Narragansett's
Zip Code on their mailbox, and remain in what appears to be
a very nice waterfront community. Sadly, if you judged him
solely by his home address, Abraham Punditt would fall under
the category of "the normal people."

Simon had said she'd send for Punditt tomorrow and call me down to talk with him when he arrived. I didn't feel like waiting that long. I had borrowed Lil's Jeep, and was parked on the end of the street on which Punditt lived. It was just past eight thirty. I'd been watching Punditt's house for a little under an hour. I could hear a baseball game winding down a couple of streets over, and the pleasant calmness of summer was settling in with the fading sunlight. If I smoked, now would be the perfect time.

I figured I'd wait until nine or nine thirty, let Punditt get comfortable, and then drop in and say hello. That plan got tossed out the window ten minutes later as Punditt came out of his house, got in his car, and backed out of his driveway. You'd never know it, the way Lil drove, but the Mustang was much faster than her Jeep. However, I didn't picture Punditt as the type to break any speed barriers in his Mercedes, so a quick decision needed to be made: follow Punditt or case his house. Trusting the influence Simon probably carried, I figured I'd still get the chance to see Abraham tomorrow. Wouldn't hurt to see what he had at home.

I waited five minutes after he left, got out of the Jeep, and locked the doors. I walked up the street to his house and knocked on the front door. Nobody answered, no dog barked.

I didn't have a crowbar, and Lil wasn't available, so I had to improvise. I walked around to the back, picked up a rock, and threw it through one of the window panes in his back door. Call me nostalgic, but sometimes the old ways are still the best.

The door opened to Punditt's kitchen and it became very apparent that aside from his car and wardrobe, Abraham didn't afford himself many luxuries. The house was lived-in, which was a huge step up from his office, but was furnished in a surprisingly modest manner. A quick walk around revealed the entire house to be one story, with a concrete basement downstairs. There were two bedrooms, one that was used as a study, a living room, eat-in-kitchen, and bathroom. The entire house was meticulously clean. Everything was orderly and put in its proper place. Breaking a widow hadn't tripped an alarm, but rearranging his bookcase probably would.

He'd left his living room lights on, so I didn't see any harm in turning the other ones on throughout the house. His house being so spartan, if I was going to find anything, it would probably be in the bedroom or the study.

The bedroom was one step away from boring. Perfectly made bed, dresser, and a closet full of clothes maybe Donald Trump could afford. I checked under the bed, rifled through drawers, checked the shelves in the closet, and found nothing. If he had any other blackmail shots, I didn't think he'd be stupid enough to store them here.

I was about to leave when I glanced at a framed picture resting on his nightstand. I picked it up to get a better look, and found myself looking at a shot of Punditt and Lindsey Oakes arm-in-arm in what seemed to be some sort of tropical resort. Lindsey was wearing an outfit that gave new meaning to the term "shorts" and was pressed up against Punditt, with her other hand resting on his chest, both of them smiling like newlyweds.

Abraham, you hound.

Who stands to profit? That's what Everett would always ask me whenever I was working on a case. I looked at the picture again and all of a sudden, things started clicking into place. I slid the picture out of the frame and put it in my shirt pocket. I placed the empty frame in his nightstand.

This was the time where if you started getting excited, you would miss something, something that would inevitably become crucial later on. I breathed through my nose to slow myself down, and began a methodical search of his study. He had two file cabinets against the far wall, and a large roll-top desk facing the window. In the interest of time, I started with the desk.

I opened the roll top up, and was greeted with the same order as the rest of the house. Cleanliness is next to godliness. His desktop calendar was blank except for the conference in Providence. Next to his calendar were some file folders. I looked through all of them, but all I found were itemized expense accounts for various tax filings.

I pulled open his desk drawer and struck gold. Tucked away on the side was a folder containing two airline tickets. The date was four days from now, and the destination was Buenos Aires. There was no return flight.

Dios mio.

I pocketed the tickets and closed up the desk. I tried one of the file cabinet doors, but they were locked. A hammer would do the trick, but that would require a return trip, and I had a pretty good idea of where I was going next. I turned off all the lights except for the living room, left through the back door, and headed back down the street.

Before we'd left Ottwain's office, Everett had asked the secretary for Bernard's files on Lindsey Norman-Oakes and Abraham. She'd hesitated for a minute, and then apparently decided if her boss had passed out in his office, he'd relinquished his authority for the day. She'd placed the two files on her desk, and then without a word, slipped out of the anteroom to check on a new pot of coffee. The files were unsurprisingly thin, but we were able to write down a home address and phone number for Lindsey and a cell for Abraham before the secretary returned. I smiled at her as we left, but she just returned a tired gaze.

Now I left Punditt's house and headed back down the street to Lil's Jeep. The night air had a cool, pleasant feel to it, one that made you not want to go indoors. I reached the car, unlocked the door, and climbed in. I could just go home, curl up with Lil, and have a drink. There was no reason to think Lucille Simon was anything but competent in her role as police officer. As a matter of fact, she probably would have Punditt in her office for the better part of the day tomorrow.

Still, it was a really nice night.

I put the airline tickets in the glove compartment and locked it. I turned the motor over, pulled off of Punditt's street, and wound my way through ten minutes of tiny side streets until I snaked back onto Route 108. Two minutes later, I was climbing the on ramp to Route 1.

Prior to the advent of multilane highways, *a la* Route 95, Route 1 was the mode of mass transit. In Rhode Island, it is still a very viable transportation option, and even at this hour, there was a moderate amount of traffic.

I drove up Route 1, and when I reached the intersection between routes 1 and 138, I pulled into the commuter lot on the side. I parked next to a large wooden structure that looked like an old-fashioned watchtower, and called the cottage. I am a failure at driving and talking on my cell at the same time, so to prevent any traffic catastrophes, I had to sit in the parking lot and wait for the other line to connect. I'm sure there was a time when private eyes relied on payphones anyway. I'd read about it in books.

Lil's voice picked up on the third ring.

"Hey."

"Hello, stranger," she said.

"I need to speak with Everett."

"Are you working?"

"Yes."

"Be careful."

Everett's voice came on the line.

"Where are you?"

"Rhode Island."

"That's specific."

"I need Lindsey's address."

If I had known my mother, I'm sure that many times she would've given me the same sigh of displeasure I now received from Everett.

"Any particular reason you're heading over there now?"

"Social call."

"Mmm. I could meet you, you know."

"Don't bother. By the time you got here, I'd probably be done anyway."

"I'm sure."

He gave me the address and I wrote it down on an envelope Lil had on the back seat. If I knew what "begrudgingly" meant, I would've understood his mood. However, since I didn't I clicked off the phone and pulled back onto Route 1 guilt-free.

I climbed up the Jamestown/Newport exit. It was past nine o'clock, the sky was clear, and a few stars shone ahead of me. I drove over the new Jamestown Bridge, which was situated right next to the old Jamestown Bridge which had not been torn down, and looked as if it simply remained there to give suicidal people something to jump off of without having to deal with the annoying flow of traffic.

I pulled off the bridge, and was immediately greeted by small, humble bungalows that dotted the streets. I suspected that Jamestown was much like Narragansett, and your status was determined by how close your house was to the water.

I drove down the road and easily forgot I was on an island. I felt like I was in the woods in Maine. Trees clustered together, filling in any empty space between the various houses. I passed a dive shop and the town library before coming to a four-way intersection. I took a left, per Everett's instructions, and within seconds, the trees disappeared and the water came into view.

I turned onto a main street that would probably classify as quaint, and passed among other things, a tiny bookstore, another dive shop, and two small restaurants that could hold maybe twenty people apiece. The buildings were the old-fashioned stone and brick, and each of them had Colonial-era signs hung on street poles outside their establishments. Two people were walking out of one of the pubs, but other than that, the street was deserted. By the looks of things, Jamestown hadn't changed since the late 1800s.

At the end of the street was a small marina, and the road curved to the left to offer a wide semicircle view of the water.

Some boats floated in the water in the marina, and across the way, I could see the lights on the Newport Bridge.

I turned the Jeep to the left and followed the road as it curved along the coast. It bore along the water, and meandered up past a large inn that sat on a shelf jutting into the sea. Everett had told me Lindsey lived on Lombard Street. However, Jamestown was not big on streetlights, and I got lost three times.

My guess about the houses on the water was proven a reality. As I drove around the neighborhood, even with the absence of light, the homes loomed overhead with the stature of old and established power. Two or three stories high, three-car garages, bay windows that stared out like empty souls, revealing nothing of what was inside. They sat with an air of established superiority, one that was acknowledged and accepted by everyone and everything in the surrounding area. It was no wonder Lindsey had chosen to make her home here.

Lombard Street was a steep hill, and as you climbed up, it became apparent that these mansions were built with the presumption of overlooking everything, including the stately manors below them. Lindsey's residence was the second from the top of the hill, an overbearing farmhouse that had been renovated to now resemble one of those old southern manses. I turned around at the top of the hill, parked the Jeep on the street, set the emergency brake, and got out.

The silence was unsettling. It was almost ten thirty, but you didn't even hear the water. I walked up Lindsey's driveway, and the crunch of the gravel underfoot seemed to echo to the other side of the state.

Abraham's Mercedes was parked in her driveway, right behind a Range Rover. I walked up the steps to her wraparound porch. There were no lights on inside. Not a sound could be heard. I reached between the railings into her flower garden, and picked up a good-sized rock. I walked back to the front of the house and heaved it through the front window closest to the door. Hey, if something works for me, I stick with it.

The silence was shattered by Lindsey's alarm system. Horns blared through the night, not only signifying an intruder, but also warning boats not to dock in her yard. I saw lights come on in the third floor windows, then the second, and then the first, followed by rapidly approaching footsteps. Abraham ripped the front door open, wearing a silk bathrobe.

"Thanks, Abe," I said, stepping in past him.

The alarm kept blaring and I expected to see a small militia appear on her front lawn. Abraham stepped over to the keypad, punched in some numbers, and the noise ceased. He was either very familiar with the house, or he was the man who was going to buy my next lottery ticket. Lindsey appeared in the living room wearing a pure white robe that was so thick with fur, I swear it moved on its own.

When she saw me, she was, again, less than thrilled. This being a look I received from many women, I remained stoically unfazed.

I looked over at Punditt.

"Consoling the bereaved widow? You really go above and beyond the call of duty."

"I hope you realize the trouble you are in right now," he said quietly.

"Try again, my friend. I think you have things a tad reversed."

Lindsey started toward me with clenched fists.

"You son of a bitch. You kill my husband and then come to my home –"

"That's enough, Lin," Punditt said, stepping in between the two of us. That annoyed me, partly because he had shut Lindsey up, but mostly because if she had a gun on her, I didn't want to have to thank Abraham for saving my life. "He's broken into your house. We'll just call the police and have him removed."

"Absolutely," I said. "Call the police, Abraham. And as they're hauling me off, I'll toss them these airline tickets you've purchased that just happen to have you and a guest leaving the country. Couple that with your prom shot," I pulled the picture out of my pocket, "and I'm sure they'll have a good idea who that guest is."

Abraham did a slow burn better than Ted Knight in *Caddyshack*. If he stomped his feet, he would've had it down cold. Lindsey wasn't so subtle.

"You cockfuck piece of shit."

"Except for 'cockfuck,' that's identical to the last sentence I heard from your sister."

This time, Lindsey did lunge at me. She didn't have a gun, but I do believe she would have clawed out my eyes if given the chance. I grabbed her by the wrists and shoved her down hard. She fell back onto the front hall staircase and stayed there looking up at me. I couldn't hold my own against Lawrence Oakes, but I could push girls around with the best of them. Abraham stayed planted where he was and told me in a sharp tone to stop it. Who said chivalry was dead?

"There's nothing criminal about airline tickets or that photo."

"Shut up," I said. "Both of you."

I was tired. I was tired of working a case that wasn't mine. Tired of people who had money and thought that automatically earned them a certain status. Tired of being poked and prodded and badgered and attacked while I was supposed to be on my vacation, goddammit.

I looked at the two of them.

"I could give a shit that the two of you are a couple. Frankly, the more I dig up about the two of you, the more I think you're made for each other. And no, Abe, that doesn't negate the fact that I still think you're gayer than Easter."

I think he flushed, but with the color of his robe matching his skin tone, it was hard to tell.

"I could give a shit that you and Erica Gold are involved in some sort of blackmail goldmine. Hell, most of those people probably have it coming. But I do know that a scared girl came to me for help and then ended up dead on my porch. Somebody needs to answer for that."

I didn't usually give speeches. I was out of breath. The two of them stared silently at me with a bewildered expression on each of their faces.

"You – you've done all of this because of Melissa? You didn't even know her."

Abraham took two steps toward me. I expected a flowery litany to pour forth, and was genuinely surprised when he was succinct and to the point.

"Mister Miller, let's put all our cards on the table, shall we? You've made reference to my past, and you've obviously worked out the scam we're running now. But don't think for a minute that either one of us would stoop to murder."

Punditt's tone was uncharacteristically blunt. There was none of his evangelical swagger, his "O Come All Ye Faithful" intonations. I had to remind myself that he was a showman. I already knew he was a criminal.

"You'll pardon me if I don't take your statement on faith."

"Crispin was going to talk." He went on like I hadn't even spoken, like he was reciting the pledge of allegiance. His gaze was fixated on me, but I had the feeling that he was looking far past me. "He was going to blow the whistle on our operation. We had pictures of him with three different hookers, the oldest one being sixteen. A thirteen-year-old giving him a blow job, a fourteen-year-old riding him backwards. He didn't care. Said he was a lawyer, he'd take care of himself. And he wasn't just going to the cops. He was calling the feds. With some of the names on our list, it actually warranted that. Well, we couldn't have that. None of us wanted it. And Erica wouldn't stand for it."

"All of a sudden Crispin just grew a pair of balls? Or all of a sudden he decided he didn't want to part with his money?"

"All of a sudden, he fell in love."

I looked over at Lindsey. "Melissa."

She nodded.

"It wasn't solely about money. Albert planned to marry her. With Melissa being his wife and my sister, he knew Erica would be merciless. He refused to bring her in and have that hanging over their heads for the rest of their lives. It was almost noble, really."

"Lawrence killed Crispin," Punditt said.

"Lawrence?"

"Volunteered for it, actually. He saw what was coming. Erica would sell us out just like she did Anthony Lucelli. No way would she have her reputation threatened. Or her money. Lawrence went over there under the guise of corroborating with Albert as a witness to protect himself, and when he got there, he shot him. Even tried to frame Melissa with the little plastic gloves."

"I didn't know about that," Lindsey said. "I didn't want my sister involved at all."

"How much was she involved?" I asked, turning back to Mrs. Oakes.

"Melissa? She was dumb as a stump. She didn't have a clue what the hell was going on."

"She was killed because of you, Miller."

"Pardon me?" I said, turning back to Punditt.

"Lawrence didn't know who you were. He just knew that you were the one who found Albert's body. He killed Melissa and left her body on your doorstep as a warning. Figured it would scare you off."

"Didn't work," I said.

I had done a very good job of bouncing my head back and forth between Punditt and Lindsey while they were talking. Always considered it bad form if you didn't look someone straight in the eye. I only had one pair of eyes though. And while I was looking at Punditt, I didn't see Lindsey get up off the staircase. And I certainly didn't see her pick the lamp up off the end table as she came up behind me. Sure as hell felt it crash into the back of my head though.

I didn't see anything after that.

I woke up face down on the floor. I didn't even open my eyes; I just lay there and tried to stop the room from spinning. I took in a sharp breath and breathed in what felt like half of Lindsey's shag carpet through my nose. I pushed myself up off the floor. The room stopped spinning and started bobbing. I felt like I was on the Tilt-a-Whirl at Disney World.

I stood up slowly, and then leaned against the wall while I waited for my eyes to focus. I reached around the back of my head and felt a sticky, dried clump that used to be the top of my neck. I looked down at the floor and saw the lamp Lindsey had used to crush in my head. The front half of the cage that held the bulb was bent in, and the bulb itself had smashed. Why did I bother to toughen up my abs?

I made my way across the hall to the living room, and sat down in one of her extravagant parlor chairs. The lights were still on, but I had no idea how much time had passed. I took a deep breath in through my nose and let it out slowly. My head was throbbing, but my vision was clear. I got up, put one foot in front of the other, and went off in search of a bathroom.

I found one nestled in between the dining room and the library, a small alcove that held two sinks, a toilet, a porcelain tub and shower stall, and a Jacuzzi. Nice to see that Lindsey kept things simple. I ran the water in one of the sinks, and washed up as best I could. I splashed some water on my face and ran it through my hair, and my head quieted down to a dull ache. Lindsey had pills galore in her medicine cabinet, but nothing that resembled aspirin.

I closed the medicine cabinet door and walked back into the foyer. Everything was quiet. I left through the front door and down the steps of the porch. Lil's car was still where I left it, but both Lindsey's and Abraham's cars were gone. I clambered into the Jeep and unlocked the glove compartment. The plane tickets were still there. I checked the clock on the dashboard. Eleven twenty. I'd been out for about forty minutes. Not much, but enough time to give the two of them a decent head start to wherever they were headed. I couldn't even be sure the two of them were traveling in the same direction.

I checked my cell phone. I had one message. I played it back, and heard Everett's voice asking me how I was doing. Just fine, Everett, I'm amazed I can still walk.

I didn't hear any sirens, nor did I see any other cars on the street. Abraham and Lindsey had simply left. Maybe I should be courteous and lock up the place for them.

I started up the engine, turned on the lights, and drove down the hill. I retraced my path back along the water and up the seventeenth-century main street. Not even midnight, and Jamestown was all but closed up.

The bridge was desolate, and I didn't start to see signs of life again until I was back on Route 1. I passed a police cruiser with its lights flashing behind a Subaru pulled over in the breakdown lane. I slowed down instinctively. One more speeding ticket and my insurance would be in the five-digit range. I thought about turning around and asking the cop if he'd seen a couple of blackmailers drive by within the last hour.

I passed the Mobil station, the courthouse, and an Applebee's, and took the exit back to Narragansett. I drove up Route 108, and against my better judgment, pulled onto the side street that led to Punditt's house. I turned onto Punditt's street and drove past his house, but the lights were off and there were no cars in his driveway or anywhere in the vicinity. Just as well. I was having trouble keeping my eyes open as I drove.

I turned around, and seven minutes later pulled the Jeep into the driveway of our rented cottage. I hadn't been here in so long, I was surprised I found my back. I pocketed Lil's keys, trudged up the stairs, and let myself in. The cottage was dark.

I made my way through the kitchen, tripped into the living room, and quietly opened the door to our bedroom.

I dropped my clothes on the floor and fell into bed. I lay on my back and didn't put up a fight as my eyelids dropped shut. I felt Lil's breath as she moved over and whispered something in my ear. I felt her kiss my cheek. I felt her rest her head on my chest.

And then I didn't feel anything.

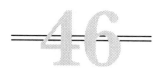

The sun streamed in through the open blinds and into the room. I glanced at the clock on the nightstand. It read ten thirty. I tried to lift my head off the pillow, but it stuck. I pulled a little harder and it came free. I looked back on the pillow and saw the dried blood. Apparently my wound had reopened during the night. I pulled on a pair of jeans and a T-shirt and walked out to the living room. Everett was doing the dishes in the kitchen, and Lil and Nicole were sitting on the deck drinking coffee.

"Helluva social call," Everett motioned at me with his head while he rinsed off a dish.

"Her version of spin the bottle," I said, running a towel under the water and applying it to the back of my head.

I patted down my neck and joined the girls on the deck. Lil put down her coffee cup and positioned my chair in front of hers. When I sat down, she pulled up behind me and inspected my cut.

"You do get all the fun, darling," Lil murmured while she gave me the once-over.

"Care to bring us up to speed?" Nicole asked.

She leaned back in her chair, held her mug on her stomach, and crossed her legs. I recounted my story, starting with the visit to Bernard Ottwain and ending with me collapsing into Lil's bed. Lil got up once during my story and returned with a bowl of warm soapy water and some gauze. She pulled two pieces of glass out before she finished dressing my wound. Apparently Lindsey could hit hard.

"So where are they now?" asked Nicole.

"No clue. I still have the plane tickets, but other than that, they could be anywhere."

Everett was leaning in the frame of the open sliding glass door that led to the deck.

"You owe it to Sergeant Simon to impart upon her the details of last night," he said. "They may have left town, but both Abraham and Lindsey are celebrities. It will be difficult for them to fade away into anonymity. The sooner she knows what's happened, the sooner she can enlist the aid of others."

"Just what I was thinking," I said as Lil finished patching me up. "Only not in so many words."

I walked out to the kitchen where I had dropped off my phone last night. I picked it up and it started to ring. I figured Lucille was psychic, but the voice on the other end was decidedly not hers.

"Miller, it's Abraham Punditt. I'm in trouble. I need help. I need to see you."

God hates me.

"Sure, Abe," I said. "How about I meet you, only this time I hand you my gun and you can shoot me instead of just whacking me on the side of the head."

"You don't understand. I need help. Lindsey went to the police this morning. She sold me out. Told them everything. She gave them proof of what we did, just left herself out of it. She sold me out."

"Where are you?"

"Mulligan's. Across from the Y. She's a murderer, Sam."

I closed my eyes. I took a deep breath.

"Don't go anywhere. I'll be there in an hour."

I hung up. This was ridiculous. What did I care if these two sold each other out? Let them shoot each other in the head for chrissakes, I could care less.

But I knew why I was going. *She's a murderer, Sam*, he had said. I had to know. And Abraham knew that, the bastard.

Mulligan's was a less-than-savory bar behind the Stop and Shop on the edge of town and across the street from the

YMCA. It had actually been my very first stop upon arriving to Narragansett. "Less-than-savory" was generous. The windows were boarded up, the inside was as dark as possible, and when you entered, the crowd knew immediately if you belonged there or not. I didn't. And when twenty-five hardened men and women turn and stare at you in a room that is midnight black at one thirty in the afternoon, that fact becomes quickly apparent. That's the problem with Rhode Island. Everybody knows everybody. And if they don't like you, you're fucked.

I walked back out to the deck.

"We need to take a ride."

"Who?"

"All of us. Punditt just got bounced by his old lady."

Everett raised his eyebrows at me.

"I know, I know. But if he's hiding –"

"As he *claims* to be –"

" – we've got a chance to put a collar on this. He was planning on leaving with Lindsey, Everett. This wasn't something spur-of-the-moment. I think they've been planning this for a while. If she's ditched him and going to the cops, he's panicking."

"Or setting you up."

"That's why you all are coming along for backup." I looked over at Lil. "Mulligan's is an old-fashioned ex-con bar. If you did time, first beer's on the house. If I go in there by myself, all eyes will be on me as the New Guy. I'll be watched and tested, and probably thrown out within five minutes. I go in there with you on my arm, I'll be automatically accepted. Maybe even respected."

Nicole shook her head.

"You'll be accepted simply because you walk in there with a nice piece of ass by your side?"

"That's about it. Image. If someone like Lil's with me, I must be doing something right. They'll respect that. Please don't give me a lecture right now on sexism and equality, OK?"

She snorted. "I could give a shit. I just want to know why I don't get to be the eye candy."

Lil got up and walked back into the house.

"Where are you going?"

"Mulligan's brings back old memories. I have to figure out what I'm going to wear."

Who stands to profit? When I was at Punditt's home, I thought I had all my ducks in a row. They might've been facing in the wrong direction.

Who stands to profit? Punditt had tickets for two out of the country. I had thought initially that the two of them would take as much money as they could and run. Their plan was quickly going down the shitter anyway.

But what if all Punditt wanted was Lindsey? That picture had been placed on his nightstand like a high school sweetheart. His house was modest and not nearly reflective of the cash he was drawing in. What did he do with his money? Of course that didn't prove anything. Maybe he was just tons smarter than Anthony Lucelli and decided not to broadcast his wealth. With his position, Abraham would be scrutinized on a daily basis anyway – an evangelist in the public eye didn't want to appear to be too wealthy.

Lindsey, on the other hand, had proven she was more of a material girl than Madonna. With Lawrence out of the way, she had access to all of his money. And if she and Punditt were going to drop out of sight and just take the money and run anyway, why not point the finger at Abraham and run off with his cash too? It made sense. The only thing left was the question of whether Abraham was dumb enough to fall for it. I'd find out soon enough, but I was pretty sure I already had my answer.

Lil and I were in the Mustang. We sped down Ocean Road and then turned onto Point Judith Road. Everett and Nicole stayed right behind us. We went through three stoplights, passed two gas stations and about sixteen donut shops. We took a left at the next traffic light, and past the Stop and Shop that sprawled across the parking lot. We turned down the second side street past the parking lot, and there on the corner, diagonally across from the YMCA, was Mulligan's.

It wasn't even noon and the parking lot was already half full. We pulled in and backed into a parking spot, making it accessible to leave in a hurry if needed. Everett pulled in alongside us.

The bright summer light did nothing but make the building look even more run down. Whatever paint had once been there had either faded or peeled off. The roof rose and fell by its own choosing, shingles nailed haphazardly with no rhyme or purpose. The sign above the door blinked on and off, regardless of the full daylight.

"Been awhile since we've been on a date," Lil said, getting out of the car.

I walked over to Everett and he rolled down his window.

"We shouldn't be in there very long. You're on speed dial. If we get in any trouble, come running as soon as your phone rings."

"Got your gun?"

"It's in the car. New Guy can't be made with a gun."

"New Guy better not get shot."

"No worries."

I tapped the roof of his car twice, and turned away toward the bar. Lil took my arm as we crossed the parking lot, and when we reached the entrance, we opened the door and walked in.

Lil was wearing a stunning backless red dress with heels to match. Initially I thought it was all for naught, as the light seemed to extinguish as soon as we entered the building. We walked the length of the bar, and the number of heads that turned coupled with the grunts of approval proved me wrong. People moved out of Lil's way as we made our way to the back of the room, smiling and nodding to her as they did so. Even ex-convicts have manners. Lucky she was still holding onto my arm; she was the only reason I had made it this far.

We got to the end corner of the bar, which was occupied by a large bald man in a ripped T-shirt, with two prison tattoos on his forearm, and an earring that resembled a baseball bat strung through his earlobe. Past him, at a table in the corner sat Abraham Punditt. He was dressed in a hooded grey sweatshirt and khakis. If he hadn't raised his left hand halfway off the table, I never would've seen him.

I slid into the booth next to Abraham, giving me a full view of the bar, and Lil moved a chair to the corner of the table, allowing her to sit with her back to the wall as well. Besides, with Abraham sandwiched between the two of us, our conversation would be all the more pleasant.

"What's going on, Abraham?" I asked, looking around the bar. "How's the missus?"

"She sold me out," he said. Both of his hands were planted on the table, and the voice came from deep within his hood. His hands were firm, but his voice shook. "She sold me out."

"Shocked," I said, looking at Lil. "Shocked, I am."

Lil gave her full-wattage smile.

"Women," she said. "You just can't trust them."

"I know," I said, rubbing the back of my neck. "I was reminded of that when she clocked me in the head."

"I didn't know she was going to do that," Abraham said.

"Neither did I."

"You scared her when you mentioned the plane tickets. She panicked. She just wanted to get out while she could. She was scared you were going to tell someone and get her in trouble. She didn't want to go to jail."

"Not many people do. She didn't take the tickets."

"We didn't know where they were. I searched you, but I couldn't find them."

"I had them in the car."

"I figured as much. By the time we were outside, her only aspiration was to get away."

If I didn't know who I was talking to, I wouldn't have believed it was Abraham Punditt. This was not a man who had stood up and dazzled legions of people last weekend at his Providence conference. This was a man beaten, a man depressed, a man who had lost. But he hadn't lost yet. The police didn't know where he was, he had called me for help, and there was still a chance of him salvaging himself by giving up Erica Gold. Punditt had played this game before. He was well aware of his options. He still had a lot left, and he knew that. Which meant he wasn't beaten over the blackmail and the money. That left one other alternative.

"Why did Lindsey turn you in, Abraham?"

"It was supposed to be storybook. Fairy tale, y'know? The two of us away forever, plenty of money and no worries."

He paused. I didn't say anything. Lil sat attentively at the end of the table, her legs crossed and head cocked to one side. Abraham continued.

"She had come to me complaining of Lawrence. He wasn't paying any attention to her. He wasn't romantic. He was never around. I could be romantic for her, I said. I would always be romantic for her. So we started seeing each other a little bit on the side. Then once in a while, we'd have an overnight, which then graduated into weekends."

I thought back to our meeting with Lindsey in the Providence hotel room. And at the hotel bar. I didn't think Lindsey had to stretch too far to find someone to pay attention to her.

"We were so good together. She'd laugh so much when she was with me. She was so happy. Lawrence never knew, and what would he care anyway? He was never home. Hell, half the time he was out snorting the coke he had salvaged from arresting Lucelli."

The hood fell back from his head, and even in the dimness, I could see that he was crying. Crying. Jesus Christ.

I flagged the waitress over to our table. She made a concerted effort to drop her cigarette ash on the floor and not on our table. I ordered a glass of wine for Lil, and a Jameson's for me. Abraham ordered a 7 and Ginger.

"She's gonna sell you down the river," I said, returning my attention to Abraham.

"I know."

"Not even a second thought."

He sighed. "I even started putting money aside. For her. My car was already paid for, and I only needed the fancy clothes for my public engagements. Everything else I put aside. I figured I could use it to treat her the way she deserved."

"She have access to the cash?"

"Yes."

"And of course, with Oakes gone, she has access to anything he left behind too."

"I think so, yes. I mean, I don't see why she wouldn't."

If I wasn't afraid of what diseases I could contract, I would've rested my head on the table out of sheer hopelessness.

"She used me."

He said the words out loud, and then the weight of what he just said dawned on him.

"She used me. Completely. Oh my God. I am such a stupid fuck."

The waitress returned with our drinks and passed them around. Lil had a large smear of lipstick around the edge of her wineglass, and after looking around, it was evident that she got the best glass of the three of us. I gave the waitress a twenty, and she walked away without even bothering to make change.

"Get used to it, Abe. Women use men. They get scared or lonely or life isn't going the way they want it, they use us."

Abraham closed his eyes, which accounted for the fact that he actually raised his glass to his lips. I waited. I felt like a heel doing it this way, but I was currently out of options. Abraham put his glass back down, and rested his forehead in his right hand.

"She killed Crispin."

There it was.

"How?"

"She has a gun. Keeps it upstairs in her vanity stand. Lawrence gave it to her. It played out just like I told you last night, only it was her, not Lawrence. She left the gloves in the garbage hoping to frame her sister. She wasn't sure how much Crispin had told her."

"What about Melissa?"

"That really was Lawrence. He wanted to scare you off, and figured Melissa was the only other person you knew here. It killed two birds with one stone as far as he was concerned. If Melissa did know anything, now she wouldn't be able to talk."

Abraham finished his drink and put his glass down. His eyes looked dull, even in the dim light.

"So what do we do?"

"Well, we could sit around and wait for Lindsey to come to her senses, realize she really does love you, burst through that door, and whisk you off to a tropical paradise. Or we could move to Plan B."

"What's Plan B?"

"Turn her in."

Abraham nodded, slowly, more to himself than to anything else. His eyes looked moist again around the edges.

"I - I really thought we were made for each other."

I looked at Lil. I looked back over at Punditt.

"Be happy you weren't."

The three of us got up and walked back down the bar to the entrance. The sunlight was blinding as we stepped back out into reality. Instinctively, I put a hand on Punditt's arm, but he didn't even try to run. He looked at the ground and walked in whatever direction we directed.

We walked over to Everett's car. I patted Abraham down.

"He's clean," I said. I opened the door and placed him in the back seat. "Take him down to Simon at the police station."

"You don't want to follow through on this?"

"You'll be a bit more welcome than me. Flash your badge. Show your authority."

"Where are you going?"

"One more loose end," I said.

"Mm-hmm," Everett said, and pulled out of the parking lot.

"There was no way I was going to bring him myself while he was crying," I said to Lil.

"I know what you mean. I never could stand to see a grown man cry."

"Yeah," I muttered. "Between the two of us, we have maybe half a heart."

Lil slapped me hard across the face.

"Don't you ever – don't you *ever* say that again when you know perfectly well it's not true. Ever."

"That makes sense," I said, climbing into the car. "If I call you heartless again, I'm going to get hit because it's a false statement."

"So what is our loose end?"

The sky had opened to display a gorgeous summer day. A couple white clouds floated above us, and the sun spread its warmth over the landscape. I put the top down on the Mustang and pulled out of the parking lot.

"You're Lindsey Oakes. You've just basically assured yourself Punditt's money as well as your dead husband's. You've even gone so far as to go to the police, probably with evidence to prove Punditt's guilt."

"Only the operation on which I'm blowing the whistle isn't my operation."

"Right. It's Erica's. So if you like your money and you want to keep it – "

"And I like my life and want to keep it – "

"You get the hell out of Dodge."

We were driving up Route 1. It was twelve fifty in the afternoon, and not much beach traffic heading home yet.

"So where do you think she'll go?"

"Don't know. We do have her two tickets to Buenos Aires in our possession."

"Think she'll come after you to get them?"

"As a last resort. I'd suspect she's in panic mode right now, trying to pack herself up quickly and quietly."

"But we don't know where she's headed."

"Which is why we're taking the fight to her, and hopefully head her off before she leaves."

"We're going to her house?"

I nodded.

"Don't know why. I vote we just go home and wait for her to come to us."

"And what if she doesn't?"

Lil made a dismissive gesture with her hand. "You're the detective."

I turned up the radio, put the car in fifth gear, and stepped on the gas.

Jamestown was a little more active in the afternoon sun than the middle of the night. People moved up and down the streets, and traffic was a mainstay all through town. The quaint little main street was busy, and the marina was filled with boats.

We drove up around the outskirts of town, and up to Lindsey Oakes's house. In the daylight, it retained its mammoth size, but the sun also showed the number of cracks and chips in its face. There was no car in the driveway as Lil and I drove on up. We parked in the driveway and walked up to the porch.

The window was still broken where I had gained entrance the day before, and no sounds emanated from within. Lil and I tried the door, and it opened right up. We walked into the foyer and turned on the lights. Nobody came charging at us with a baseball bat or shooting at us from the top of the stairs. We were alone.

"I don't think anyone's here," Lil said.

"Think you're right. Wanna make out?"

"Why don't we make sure first," she winked.

We searched through the first floor. No one was there, and everything appeared undisturbed. We crept up the stairs to the second floor. We found a second dining room, an exercise room, and an entertainment room with a TV bigger than our cottage, again all undisturbed.

"Where's her bedroom?" asked Lil.

"Third floor."

"You answered that way too quickly."

We climbed to the third floor. No one appeared at the top of the staircase wielding a shotgun, and no one jumped out from the shadows with a kitchen knife.

"What are we looking for?"

"No self-respecting woman would leave town without packing some clothes. Show me her bedroom, and I can tell you whether she's still in Rhode Island."

The third room we entered had to be her bedroom. It was massive. A full canopy bed filled the center, and six closets adorned the walls. Two full bureaus with three mirrors apiece graced the opposite end of the room, and two full baths were built off the side. Lil went to work on the closets while I searched the drawers in the bureaus.

"There's no way in hell to tell if she took any clothes, but there are no suitcases in any of the closets."

"Her gun's still here," I said, shutting the drawers. Lil came over, picked it up, and dropped it in her purse. "What do we do?"

"Stay here and see if she returns?"

"No. If she was going to take anything, she's already come and gone. We've missed her."

Lil's cell phone rang. She dug it out of her purse and answered it.

"It's Everett," she said. "The police are holding Abraham overnight. If we don't need him for anything, he's taking Nicole out to a production of Shakespeare in the Park down in Westerly."

"Tell him we're all set."

"He says we're welcome to come along."

"Shakespeare. You feel like translating for me?"

"Not particularly."

"Tell him thanks anyway."

She spoke into the receiver and hung up.

"We did the best we could, babe."

"Mmmm."

"We got farther than the police did."

"Yep."

"It wasn't even your case."

"I know."

She came over and kissed me above my left eye.

"Let's go home."

We turned off the lights, closed the front door, and walked out to the car. I tossed Lil the keys. She got in the driver's side, fired up the car, and pulled away from the curb. She got us home ten minutes quicker than I did the other night.

And this time, we had to fight the traffic.

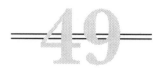

The sun wasn't even thinking about setting when we arrived back in Narragansett. Lil pulled into the driveway and put the top up. We could hear the lifeguard's voice carry up from the beach.

We got out of the Mustang and walked up the stairs. I opened the door and walked in, Lil right behind me. She shut the door. When she turned around, we were both looking at Lindsey Norman-Oakes in our living room.

Christ Almighty, we don't even live in this town and everyone knows our address.

Lil looked at me.

"Told you."

"Afternoon, asshole," Lindsey said, and pointed a gun at us.

"You're in my chair," I said.

"Sit down," she said, and motioned to the couch with the gun.

I walked into the living room. Lil went to the fridge.

"Hey," she called in to Lil. "In here!"

Lil had grabbed a pitcher of iced tea out of the fridge. She closed the fridge with her free hand and set the pitcher on the countertop.

"Relax, darling," she said, placing three glasses on a tray. "If we're going to do this, we can at least do it like civilized people."

She carried the tray and the pitcher out to the living room. She placed the tray on the coffee table and poured a glass.

"You do that like a professional," I said.

She smiled. "Would anybody care for a glass?"

Lindsey tried her best to give Lil a menacing look.

"Suit yourself," Lil said, and sank back into the sofa.

"Give me your purse," Lindsey said.

Lil tossed her purse at Lindsey's feet. She picked it up awkwardly, holding the gun on us while she reached down to grab it. She dumped the contents out onto the carpet. When she came across her gun, she looked up at us. Lil smiled at her.

"What can we do for you, Lindsey?" I asked. "Have you come to turn yourself in?"

"I'll hand it to you, you prick. You've done a pretty good job of fucking up my entire operation here. This one was working very well for me."

"Let's give credit where credit is due, Lindsey," I said. "With all due respect, it's Erica's operation. You're just her errand girl."

"Arrogant," she smirked. "I might just kill you second, just for fun. Make you watch me kill your little girlfriend."

She stood up and kept the gun pointed in our direction. She walked in a half circle around the other side of the coffee table so that she ended up away from me and next to Lil. Lindsey was dressed in casual attire, a warm-up jacket, sweatpants, and flip-flops. Either this was an outfit on which she didn't mind getting blood, or one she planned on throwing out.

"This is Erica Gold's gun," she said as she walked. "Grabbed it early this morning when I left her bed."

Erica really was your all-around girl.

"I wanted to make sure after you two were dead I'd be left alone. While the cops are pestering Erica why she shot you and then comparing her story with Abraham, I'll be long gone."

"Would you care for the tickets?" I asked. Anything to keep her talking.

"Buenos Aires was Abraham's idea," she said. "I was always a Caribbean girl myself. Erica purchased two tickets anonymously through her firm for our anniversary, the day after tomorrow. I'll just use the empty seat to store my carry-on bag."

She stepped around and pressed the muzzle of the gun up against Lil's temple.

"On your feet, girlie."

Lil stood. With one hand, Lindsey kept the gun leveled at Lil's head, and she wrapped the other arm around Lil's neck, pulling her close in front of her.

"Loose ends," she smiled. "I just can-"

Lil drove the spike of her heel into the bridge of Lindsey's foot. Lindsey shrieked in pain. Lil was wearing her stilettos. It's all about the style.

The two of them went down together, and I dove off the couch onto Lindsey's gun. Lil drove her elbow straight back into Lindsey, and I backhanded her across the face. I stood up with her gun in my hand. Lil stood up, kicked Lindsey once in the ribs, smoothed out her dress, and sat down.

"Bitch," she said to no one in particular, and poured herself another glass of iced tea.

Lindsey pulled herself up and looked at me. She quietly smoothed her hair. She glanced around the room, found a stool, pulled it over and sat down. She looked back up at me.

"Let's remember you're the good guy, Miller," she said.

"That's the same thing your husband said. Right before I broke his neck."

Her eyes got a little wider.

"Let's be rational here," she said. "We can split the cash."

"You threatened Lil."

"I can help you take down Erica. The press will love you. The state will love you. And we can still split the cash."

"You killed Melissa."

"No, I didn't. That was Law-"

"You don't get it, sweetie," Lil said. Her voice didn't betray a hint of emotion or aggravation. She spoke in a soft, casual rhythm. A matter-of-fact tone. Almost bored. "He doesn't quit. He's a bulldog. He won't stop until the job is done. No shortcuts. Stubborn. Determined. Sadly, it's his most endearing trait."

"She's just being generous," I said. "I'd just as soon shoot you."

I raised my arm and put a bullet through the wall above her head.

Lindsey looked like she was about to be sick, and then fainted to the floor.

I looked at Lil.

"Better get the spackle if we plan to come back here next year."

About the Author

Marc Blevins is, among other things, a bartender, a real estate salesperson, and a high school English teacher. He graduated from the University of Rhode Island in 1995 with a degree in Secondary Education and English. He has spoken at Hawaii's International Conference on Arts and Humanities on the evolution of detective fiction. He lives in Rhode Island. If you stop in the right bar, he might even buy you a beer.

Printed in the United States
69970LV00010B/64-75

9 781420 874433